To

911 by Chris Owen
An Agreement Among Gentlemen by Chris Owen
Bareback by Chris Owen
The Broken Road by Sean Michael
Cowboy Up edited by Rob Knight
Deviations: Domination by Chris Owen and Jodi Payne
Deviations: Submission by Chris Owen and Jodi Payne
Don't Ask, Don't Tell by Sean Michael
Fireline by Tory Temple
Historical Obsessions by Julia Talbot
Jumping Into Things by Julia Talbot
Landing Into Things by Julia Talbot
Latigo by BA Tortuga
Locked and Loaded edited by SA Clements
Music and Metal by Mike Shade
Need by Sean Michael
On Fire by Drew Zachary
Out of the Closet by Sean Michael
Perfect by Julia Talbot
Personal Leave by Sean Michael
Rain and Whiskey by BA Tortuga
Redemption's Ride by BA Tortuga
Secrets, Skin and Leather by Sean Michael
Shifting, Volumes I-III, edited by Rob Knight
Tempering by Sean Michael
Three Day Passes by Sean Michael
Timeless Hunger by BA Tortuga
Tomb of the God King by Julia Talbot
Touching Evil by Rob Knight
Tripwire by Sean Michael
Tropical Depression by BA Tortuga
Under This Cowboy's Hat edited by Rob Knight

Secrets, Skin and Leather

This is a work of fiction. Names, characters, places, and incidents either are the product of the author's imagination or are used fictitiously. Any resemblance to actual events, locales, organizations, or persons, living or dead, is entirely coincidental and beyond the intent of either the author or the publisher.

Secrets, Skin and Leather
TOP SHELF
An imprint of Torquere Press Publishers
PO Box 2545
Round Rock, TX 78680
Copyright © 2005, Sean Michael
Cover illustration by Rose Meloche
Published with permission
ISBN: 1-934166-55-3, 978-1-934166-55-0
www.torquerepress.com
All rights reserved, which includes the right to reproduce this book or portions thereof in any form whatsoever except as provided by the U.S. Copyright Law. For information address Torquere Press.
First Torquere Press Printing: December 2006
Printed in the USA

   If you purchased this book without a cover, you should be aware the this book is stolen property. It was reported as "unsold and destroyed" to the publisher, and neither the author nor the publisher has received any payment for this "stripped book".

Prologue

Dillon Walsh sat back, watching the other men around the table, listening to the proceedings with half an ear.

Three brokers, two company presidents, a handful of vice-presidents, and an assorted variety of lawyers, all haggling about who was going to get what as Watson Towers and Bellamy Inc. were merged into one of the umbrella corporations that Dillon's company oversaw.

He was richer than God, and probably just as bored.

And there wasn't a man here worth his attention.

Biting back his sigh, Dillon poured himself a glass of water.

He imagined old Sam Williamson in a leather-daddy outfit and actually had to bite the side of his mouth to keep from laughing out loud. The old man would probably be happier all trussed up licking someone else's boots.

Taking a sip of his water, he turned his attention to the young broker next to the old geezer.

Dark hair, dark eyes, thin lips held tight together -- the lean little shit looked like he'd never laughed or fucked or anything but made money and gone to church.

Secrets, Skin and Leather

Dillon put him in the leather-daddy outfit and snorted, lips twitching as eight sets of eyes turned on him, the broker -- another fucking "s" name: not Sam, but Steve? Simon? Scotty? -- looking like he'd be the first to call the men in white coats.

"I don't think you need me at this point, do you? I have other business to attend to." He fixed each one of them with a hard look, saving Prim-and-Proper-Boy for last.

"I'm sure we can have the proper paperwork faxed to you." Proper Boy had a hint of southern accent, the barest hint of impatience there.

"At least one of you will." He closed his laptop, put it into his briefcase, and then snapped the case closed.

He looked them all over again, gaze lingering on Proper Boy. He wondered briefly what it would be like to get that stiff back to unbend, what it would take to ruffle those uptight feathers.

"Well then, if there's nothing else..."

"Have a good afternoon, Walsh. I'm sure we'll manage." Katherine Fents dismissed him with a wave, the men all turning back to the table.

He was sure they would.

He had one last glance as he left, eight backs as stiff as each other.

He rolled his eyes as the doors closed behind him.

He needed a hobby.

***

Dillon leaned back against the bar, a whiskey, neat, in his hand.

He'd been to the Golden Scabbard once or twice before. When he was bored, when the suits at work got to be too much and he needed to be out with people who knew how to have fun, how to let go.

The Scabbard hosted a wide variety of people, and in just a glance he took in goth boys and transvestites, leather-daddies with their boytoys, punks, sluts.

His own outfit of tight leather pants and a T-shirt was tame here, but it let him more or less blend in and just enjoy the view.

And what a view he had. The man he was looking at was stunning, wearing a pair of skin-tight, tissue-paper-thin jeans and a black leather cincher around his waist. The man's eyes were kohled, nipples rouged and hard.

Dillon's cock, at half mast since he'd walked in, slowly started to fill, pushing against the leather ties that held his pants closed.

He took a mouthful of his drink, eyes scanning the rest of the room in a slow perusal before coming back to the sexy minx in the cincher. The man was lean, broad shoulders tightening down into a perfect, tiny ass. A perfect, tiny ass that shook to the music like it was made for it.

Groaning, Dillon dropped his hand to his thigh, working hard to keep from sliding it along his prick.

His prick. That he could imagine plowing into

Secrets, Skin and Leather

that perfect little ass.

He started working out his game plan to make it happen.

Someone came up, kissed Mr. Perfect Ass good and hard before continuing on, leaving the group of men dancing together laughing and hooting. Oh, yeah, he wanted a piece of that. A nice, long, hard fuck.

He finished his whiskey and put the glass back on the bar, still watching, focused now. There was something familiar about the shape of Perfect Ass' jaw... Dark spiky hair, bright light blue eyes, lush laughing mouth -- where had he seen that face?

He ordered another drink, trying to work it out before he went to make his move and secure his entertainment for the night.

Come on, Dillon, look past the kohl, figure it out...

It was the way the light fell, shadowing the bright eyes and making the smiling face suddenly sharp-edged, stern.

Jesus Christ.

It was Mr. Stick-Up-His-Ass Proper Boy from the merger meeting he'd ditched earlier in the day.

No fucking way.

His eyes narrowed. Yes, fucking way. That was exactly who it was.

Who the Hell knew that prim and proper demeanor, the uptight face and stern business suits hid this?

Another man came up, took a kiss, hand

putting a tiny silver clamp on one tight nipple.

No. No, that was his.

The surety of his thoughts surprised him. He came here and to other places like it for a quick fix of his boredom. For one-night stands. He never came here for more. But something told him he wanted this one for more than one night. Something in the way that tiny ass shook and those little nipples begged for more attention than just a clamp.

A new plan began to form in his head. One that included not only sliding into the sweet ass beneath the cincher, but debauching the prim and proper businessman as well.

Dillon finished his drink and slipped out of the club, riding the anticipation like a drug.

Secrets, Skin and Leather

Chapter One

Scott leaned down over his paperwork, staring at the topics that were going to be covered over the conference. Most of them were average, boring, but he could be bored for four free nights in paradise. The little island was beautiful, secluded. The hotel was five-star, the food luscious. If he hadn't had to be here as Scott Daly, stick-in-the-mud extraordinaire? It would be perfect.

Long, manicured fingers covered the paper in his hands, a soft chuckle sounding. "This is cocktail hour. Time to meet and greet, not worry about business. Mr. Daly, isn't it?"

He looked up to find Mr. High-and-Mighty Dillon Walsh himself smiling down at him.

Scott blinked up, almost smiled back. Almost. "Mr. Walsh. How very nice to see you here. Are you looking forward to the conference?"

Walsh's smile turned predatory and his dark eyes lit up. "Indeed, Mr. Daly. I am. Now, what can I get you to drink?"

"Oh, I believe I'll have a club soda." Scott Daly didn't drink. Ever.

One eyebrow went up. "A club soda? Mr. Daly, you're on a tropical island. Why not live a little?" Man, Dillon Walsh had a low, deep voice. It vibrated between them.

If you only knew, tall, dark and handsome.

"Oh, I am here on business, after all."

Walsh's chuckle sounded again. "You're on an island paradise and all you can think of is business. I knew you were a stickler, Mr. Daly, but I didn't realize just how much of one you were. I was hoping that this evening's mixer would help us all get to know each other a little better."

Because you could so handle getting to know me. God, he was bored. "I suppose one drink will suit. I would hate to offend."

"Excellent." Walsh's eyes traveled from his eyes to his shoes and back up again. "Let me guess. Vodka and orange?"

Tequila, pretty boy. Straight up. "That sounds perfect."

"You see? We're already getting to know each other better."

Walsh ordered the vodka and orange, and a whiskey neat for himself. A moment later they were joined by two men who were introduced as brokers from one of Walsh's umbrella corporations. And the "mixer" went from boring to downright dull.

He sipped and listened with half an ear, reminding himself of his bank account, his loft, his Mercedes. He had left Houston and the nightlife for a reason.

Cash in hand, baybee.

Really, though, sometimes he wanted more.

He found Walsh's eyes on him several times. He wondered if Walsh was scoping them all out during this little conference. The man certainly

Secrets, Skin and Leather

always seemed to have his fingers in every pie. Finally, *finally*, Walsh took his leave and the rest of them followed the top dog's lead, slowly drifting away.

He waited until he was alone, then went to a house phone, dialing the bar. "I need a bottle of Cuervo delivered to cabin 13, please."

"Yes, sir. Would you like salt and lime as well?"

"Yes, that would be perfect."

It was quiet on his way from the main building to his cabin, a luscious sunset painting the sky with deep velvet blues and purples. The breeze from the ocean was fresh and clean, warm. The path stayed free of other guests right up to his own door where he was met by a room service clerk, a young man with tanned skin and dark hair, warm eyes and a ready smile.

Oh, pretty pretty. Wanna come in and share a bottle, sweet thing? He smiled back. "You, dear sir, are my own personal savior."

The guy beamed at him, taking the keycard from his fingers and opening the door for him. "Is there anything else you need, sir?"

If he wasn't here for business, he'd have a fucking laundry list, washing to starch.

"Not tonight." He looked around, then didn't take the chance. "Maybe later."

"Very well, sir." The bottle was handed over to him, the waiter pocketing his tip with a smooth, practiced move. "If you ask for Ricky, I would be happy to serve you."

"Ricky." He held those pretty eyes for a

moment. "I'll remember."

Down, boy.

No seducing the locals.

Working. Workingworkingworking.

He was given another beaming smile, and then Ricky took off down the path, tray swinging.

He took his Cuervo into the room, turning on the light. The room was simple, but elegant, dominated by a large bed with mosquito netting around it. His eyes were drawn to a gold-wrapped package sitting in the middle of the white comforter.

Scott locked the door and headed over, fingers working the neck of the tequila bottle. What the Hell...

He took his tie off before sitting to unwrap the package, looking for a tag, a hint.

Something.

There was a small gold card on the underside of the package, the script inside sharp, bold. "Wear it for me."

Scott's eyebrows drew closer together. Wear it? Wear what? What the fuck...

He opened the box, lips parting as he reached in, pulled the contents out.

Oh, fuck him raw.

It was a cincher. Pristine white leather with long, long threads to pull it closed.

It looked fucking expensive. Fucking sexy.

Who the Hell had sent it? Who the fuck had found him out? God. God. Fuck.

He stood up, started panicking. He should

Secrets, Skin and Leather

pack up, feign illness and leave. Just head home. Now.

Right fucking now.

His eyes were drawn to the leather, over and over, the tequila bottle dangling from his fingers.

The phone rang, startling him with its shrill bell.

Fuck.

Fuck.

Fuck fuckety fuck fuck fuck.

He schooled his face, caught sight of his eyes, still covered in the dark contacts, in the mirror, and picked up the phone.

"Yes?"

"Mr. Daly? It's Dillon Walsh. I wanted to make sure you'd received the new schedule. The mergers meeting has been moved to ten o'clock tomorrow, and I think you should be there. You would add a lot to the meeting."

"I... I hadn't, no. Thank you for the update. Which room?" He could always leave after, just out of curiosity.

"Meeting room three. I'd also like to invite you to dinner tomorrow evening." Walsh's voice lowered, became more... intimate. "I believe you and I have a lot we could learn from each other. And my top executives, of course."

"Of course, Mr. Walsh. I'd be delighted." Assuming he didn't just die from sheer fucking panic.

"Excellent." There was a slight pause, and then that deep voice continued. "I hope you found everything in your room to your liking,

Mr. Daly?"

"Pardon me?" He looked over to the bed again, heart racing.

"Your cabin, Mr. Daly -- is it satisfactory?"

"It is. Yes. Quite. Quite fine, thank you."

All except for that...

That.

That beautiful, sexy, fucking hot corset waiting for him.

Christ.

"Good. Please do let me know if you need anything. I believe you'll find that I'm a very amenable host. Sleep well, Mr. Daly."

"Thank you. Pleasant dreams." He unscrewed the top of the tequila bottle.

"They will be," murmured Walsh, and then the line went dead.

Dal hung the phone up and stopped to remove his contact lenses, his jacket, his tie, before drinking his first two shots.

All the time he stared at the box on the bed.

By the time he had it laced up, squeezing him tight, making his skin look so fine, his cock was deep red and leaking.

Oh, fuck him raw.

***

Dillon buttered his roll, enjoying the breeze blowing off the ocean.

The sun shone into the alcove of the private dining room, warming the silverware on the table set for two. It was quiet and peaceful and perfect.

Secrets, Skin and Leather

His little two-day conference had ended, and he'd had the executives and businessmen ferried off the island bright and early. Some fiction about the planes from the mainland all leaving by nine AM.

It left only the staff, himself and Scott Daly at the resort. He grinned at the thought of Daly, the corners of his mouth pulling up in a wide smile. He'd left gifts in the man's room. One for each night. A corset the first night, a cock ring the second, and two little silver nipple clamps last night.

He'd spent the entire first day of the conference hard, all but wiggling in his seat as he imagined Daly wearing the corset beneath his prim, no-nonsense button down business suit. The anticipation was thrumming through him still. Today was the day. Today he would confront Daly, let the man know that his secret had been discovered. That Dillon *knew*.

He took a bite of his roll, the pastry flaky and sweet, butter the perfect accent. It was as if everything had taken on new life, become sharper, his interest in each little thing become keener.

Scott Daly walked in, lean and fit, body taut under the conservative, stiff, unflattering suit, eyes a dull brown. "Good morning. Am I early?"

Dillon took a deep breath. He swore he could smell Scott's scent on the breeze as it billowed the gauze curtains.

"Not at all; you're just in time." He pointed toward the chair across from him.

Daly sat slowly, posture perfect, lips full, fine.

Dillon could picture those lips as they were that night at the Scabbard, the same full, fine look, only redder, slightly swollen from passionate kisses from other men. Strangers, perhaps, Daly opening himself up so beautifully.

Dillon licked his lips. "Tell me, what do you think of my little island paradise?"

"It is quite charming. The staff is very accommodating." A piece of toast was taken, nibbled.

"And most discreet," Dillon added. His eyes met Daly's, held them.

One eyebrow arched, lips tightening a bit. "Always an exceptional quality in an employee."

"Indeed." He wanted to ruffle those fine, button down feathers. He licked his lips, took a breath and spoke softly. "Are you wearing it?"

"Pardon me?" Those fake-colored, covered eyes went wide.

"Yes, I guess I should be more specific." There had, after all, been three gifts. "I imagine you look stunning in white." Not that the black cock ring or silver nipple clamps wouldn't look stunning, as well, but it was the cincher he'd been imagining at night when he took himself in hand.

"I... I'm sure I don't know what you're talking about." Wow, Daly was good. How many years of repression was needed to keep that innocent look on his face?

"No?" He let an eyebrow rise and then

dropped his gaze to Daly's waist, trying to see through the dark jacket. He slowly let his eyes come back to meet Daly's.

"No." He could almost feel the man's heat.

He bit back his smile and reached for the pot of coffee, offering to pour a cup for Daly as he tried to decide what his next move should be.

"Where is everyone? They'll miss out on breakfast."

He poured out the coffee for Daly. "They weren't invited to breakfast."

Picking up a Danish, he tore off a piece and offered it over with his fingers. "You really must try these. I've never tasted one quite like it."

Daly reached out, took the piece, fingertips barely touching his own. "Thank you."

"My pleasure," he murmured, his eyes drifting back to Daly's waist. "Your suits are always such a conservative dark blue, or black. It makes me wonder how often they hide treasures."

"Treasures?" Oh, pretty, what big eyes you have.

"Oh, yes. Treasures large and small." He waited a moment and then added a single word. "Tight."

The coffee cup clattered to the saucer, Daly's napkin fluttering down. "I believe I'm finished, thank you."

"Stay, Mr. Daly. Our conversation is only just beginning to get interesting. And I have hope that you will answer my original question."

"I... I have no idea which question that is."

One hand rested flat on that tight stomach.

Oh, yes.

He could just imagine how Daly looked, the white corset pulled tight, the tiny, perfect ass beneath it. Dillon's cock was hard in his pants, throbbing with his pulse. He didn't want to use his imagination, he wanted to see if reality matched it. Bettered it.

"Are you wearing it?" he repeated slowly, holding Daly's eyes, not letting the man look away.

"Yes." The word fell between them, bald and quiet and just what he needed to hear.

Then Daly stood and walked away from the table. He could see it now, in the way the man moved, the way the tight corset gave him a sensuous, careful grace. Groaning, Dillon stood and dropped his napkin over his plate, then hurried to join Daly along the path back to cabin thirteen.

"So you appreciated my gifts then."

"What do you want?"

"I would have thought that was obvious, my dear Daly -- I want you." He didn't see any point in pretending. He'd bought Daly gifts, brought him to this paradise, arranged for their privacy. He wanted this man. Or, rather, the man that lurked beneath the contacts and the suit and the false prudery.

The door to the room was opened, Daly stepping right in, the evidence of his gifts there, as well as toys, tequila. Mussed sheets. He could smell Daly in here. Smell the scent of need and

Secrets, Skin and Leather

want and come.

He stepped in with the man and closed the door, reaching behind himself to turn the lock. "I want to see."

"People in Hell want ice water." Oh. Look at Daly vibrate.

"And when I'm in Hell *I* will have it." He undid his tie and pulled it from his shirt collar.

Daly's eyes watched him, just fastened on his hands. He undid the top button of his shirt, unfastened the one holding his suit jacket closed. He was nearly vibrating himself, need clawing at his spine. "Show me."

"This can't fucking be real." Oh, fuck. Listen to the drawl, the pure sex. The difference.

His cock jerked. He could smell himself now, his own need scenting the air like a cat in heat. "Feels pretty damned real to me. Now, I won't tell you again. Show. Me." He would not be denied. Not after fantasizing over this since he'd first seen the man all tricked out.

The long fingers opened the dark jacket first, then the buttons on that perfectly white shirt. Muscled and tanned and smooth, Daly's torso made his mouth water, the white leather wrapped tight around that flat belly made him ache.

"Oh, sweet Christ." He swallowed, hands curling into fists at his sides to keep from reaching out and touching. Not yet. Not, quite yet.

He licked his lips. "Take the jacket and shirt right off, Daly."

"You seem to believe I take orders." God, the

man smelled so good. Hot.

"It isn't personal, Daly. I believe *everyone* takes orders." From employees to friends to lovers. Giving orders was simply a function of who Dillon was. "What I believe is that you wish -- no, that you *need* -- to be seen."

"How did you find out?" The jacket was removed, hung carefully in a closet.

"I *see* you." It wasn't a lie.

The shirt went next, giving him a nice long look at Daly's back, waist, amazing ass.

Dillon couldn't restrain his moan, his whole body going tight at the sight. Was Daly wearing underwear beneath the expensive slacks, or would Dillon have an unfettered view of the man's ass when his trousers went the way of his shirt and jacket?

"Continue," he murmured, voice rough, throaty.

"Who the fuck told you?" Daly stepped out of his shoes, muscles tight, tense.

He shook his head, eyes on the pretty pink nipples. They were unadorned, neither rouged as they had been that night, nor wearing the little silver clips he'd had left on Daly's bed the night before. "No one told me."

The socks went next, brown eyes staring over at him, expressionless and still.

"Your eyes are wrong," Dillon said softly. "You can't go halfway. You need me to see it all." He needed to see it all.

"You saw me. Somewhere out playing." That fact seemed to relax Daly, seemed to settle him somehow, and he headed across the floor toward the bathroom.

"Clever, clever boy," he murmured, following, lounging against the doorjamb. He could see himself in the mirror, see how calm and in control he looked; only his voice had betrayed his excitement.

Daly wasn't the only one who wore masks.

"I am." The contacts were removed, then those fingers ruffled the tightly controlled and styled hair, leaving Daly looking rumpled and fuckable.

Those amazing blue eyes met his, hungry and wicked and playful, and just a little pissed. "Better?"

It was the most delicious transformation. That fire and passion was heady, and as arousing as the sight of the corset tied so tightly around Daly's waist.

He shrugged out of his jacket and hung it on the bathroom doorknob. "Yes, much." He let his eyes travel along the length of Daly's body, the black slacks incongruous with the rest of the picture. He licked his lips. "Almost perfect, in fact."

Daly's chin lifted, hands sliding down the lean body, caressing, showing off. "Almost?"

"Yes, almost." The words were almost growls, his cock pressing at his zipper, tenting his own oh-so-expensive suit pants. He'd never seen anything so lovely, so arousing. Dillon's whole body was tight, waiting for the final reveal.

"I don't get to see yours?" Those hands were at Daly's waistband, the button undone, the barest hint of dark curls exposed.

"All things in time." His eyes were locked onto that patch of skin, willing Daly to continue, to expose the whole package.

The fly opened, that long, bare cock heavy and turgid, pushing out for him to see. Then Daly turned, pushed the slacks down and off, giving him that fine, hard little ass, the muscles framed by the cincher strings.

"Oh, fuck." Groaning he took a step forward and then another, hands out, reaching for the perfect globes.

Daly stepped forward, just out of reach. "You next."

He groaned again, fingers closing on air.

"Undress me," he ordered.

"Bossy, bossy." Daly licked those pretty, bee-stung lips, eyes dragging over him. "Do you always get what you want?"

"I do." And he wanted Daly. Badly. Wanted to bury himself between those beautiful cheeks, wanted to play with those pretty little nipples, suck that gorgeous full cock.

His shirt was unbuttoned, Daly's fingers never touching his skin, just constantly teasing.

He breathed in deeply, pulling in the musky, male scent that rose from Daly's body. He could feel the warmth pouring from all that lovely skin as well, and it was all he could do not to reach out and touch. He was not a man to deny himself, but he knew that in this case, the delay could only increase the promised pleasure to come.

"Tease," he accused softly, eyes running over Daly's so-close body.

"Yes." Daly's eyes smiled at him, hands pushing the shirt down over his shoulders.

He chuckled, hissing just a little as the cool ocean air slid over his skin as it was exposed. It made the heat coming off Daly stronger.

"You aren't a pushover." It was a compliment. He liked the fire in Daly's eyes, the strength in the man's limbs.

"No. Not even a little." No, what Dillon got from this man would be given because Daly needed it, wanted it. Took it.

His slacks were unbuttoned. "Take your shoes off."

He breathed deeply, body pushing toward Daly's hands. He toed the heels off his fancy patent leather oxfords, kicking them out of the way, the movement pushing his hips forward.

"So, you were in one of my worlds, so you like to play..." Daly eased his slacks down, body moving to some internal song. "The nipple clamps were lovely. I almost hoped for a nice heavy plug for tonight, something to stretch me."

"Patience, Daly, the gifts always arrived at the end of the day, yes? And in the meantime," he looked down at his own cock. It pushed eagerly from his body, hard, tip leaking, large vein throbbing with his heartbeat. It was a testament to how sexy Daly was in the cincher, to how turned on Dillon was. "I believe I have something that will do."

"Dal." Those long fingers trailed up along his cock, petting and stroking.

He swallowed, tongue coming out to lick his suddenly very dry lips. He managed to keep his hips still, to let Daly take the lead. For now. "What?"

"They call me Dal, the people that know me." One finger pressed into his slit, making it burn, just enough.

"Dal!" He gasped, back arching, hands coming out to hold onto Daly's -- Dal's -- biceps. "I like it. You may call me Dillon."

"Hey, Dillon, nice to meet you." Dal leaned close, tongue sliding along his bottom lip, hot as Hell.

"Likewise," he muttered, closing the scant distance between their mouths and melding them together. His fingers tightened on Dal's arms as his own tongue met and danced with Dal's. The kiss went deep and hard immediately, the hunger between them razor-sharp. Dal's body was heated, the line of leather around his middle cooler, distracting.

Their cocks slid together, making Dillon moan, the sound coming from somewhere deep inside him. His hands slid from Dal's arms to his back and slowly, so very slowly, moved down searching for the corset. Christ, it was a tease, to both of them, and so good.

The line from broad shoulder to tiny waist fascinated him, the way the cincher squeezed drawing his fingers. His thumbs slid along the front of the cincher, tracing the bone insets and threaded patterns. The rest of his fingers slid along Dal's back, swept slowly down toward Dal's ass. The laces strained, the curve of Dal's back made perfect and arched by the boning.

He sucked Dal's tongue into his mouth, taking over the kiss as his fingers slid down the curve and up over Dal's ass cheeks. They fit perfectly in his hands. Dal arched, ass pushing into his touch, the man as eager and seductive and limber as he had been that night in the club.

He fingered the ties, tugging them, spreading them over Dal's ass and then pushing them aside so he could run his thumbs along Dal's crack. His own cock throbbed, dripping, making both his and Dal's cocks slick with his wanton need. Dal's ass squeezed and rocked, the muscles tight and strong, promising an amazing ride, an amazing grip around his cock.

"I want you," he told Dal, looking into those wicked blue eyes. "I want to bend you over and watch my cock slide into your ass, feel the leather ties sliding on my skin as I fuck you."

"You have rubbers?"

"In the drawer of your bedside table. There's lube in there as well." And perhaps a few other toys as well. The staff had been instructed to stock it as soon as Dal'd left his room for breakfast this morning.

"Impressive. What if I'd been the wrong man?" Dal pulled away, turned and walked toward the bed, ass swaying, just so.

"You weren't," Dillon answered, following

that ass, eyes riveted to the way the corset framed it, to the way the ties came down over it, sliding back and forth with each step.

Then Dal bent to dig in the bottom drawer, thighs just spread and...

Oh.

Oh, fuck.

Two silver rings -- one behind the other, buried in the man's perineum.

"You naughty, naughty boy." Groaning, he closed the space between them and went to his knees, hands sliding around Dal's hips, holding them in his palms as he bent to breathe on the metal.

The skin tightened, moving the rings. The scent was heady, the heat enough to make him flushed and feverish. Dal braced against the end table, spread wider. "I have lots of little secrets, Dillon."

"And I will take pleasure in discovering each and every one, Dal." Dillon breathed in deeply and then pressed his nose to Dal's perineum, tongue sliding through the rings. He got a deep, raw little sound, Dal going up on tip-toe. Beautiful. Just beautiful. He could grow to need sounds like that. He dragged his tongue through the rings, the heat of Dal's skin like a fire. He wet and twisted the rings, using his tongue to tug them down, stretching Dal's skin.

"Oh. Oh, you're a natural. A gem. Harder. Let me feel it."

He growled a little to let Dal know he'd heard and grabbed one of the rings with his teeth,

Secrets, Skin and Leather

tugging hard.

"Fuck!" Dal jerked, entire body arching, begging for him. Hell, yes. Just like that.

He pulled on the ring again and then licked at the skin it was attached to before treating the other ring to the same hard tugs. It was amazing that such passion and need could be kept so hidden within the confines of a business suit and prudish attitude.

It was even more amazing that he'd discovered it.

Dal reached down, starting stroking that long cock, skin slapping against skin.

He growled again and pulled back to bite hard on Dal's ass, hard enough to leave a mark. To leave his mark bright and red on the perfect ass cheek. "You'll get it up again?"

"I don't know. I came three times last night, once early this morning, but I'll sure try."

"Four times..." He groaned. "You liked my gifts."

He reached for the rings with his fingers this time, grabbing them and twisting them. The fingers of his other hand spread Dal's crease, and he dove in, tongue laving the wrinkled little hole.

"Oh. Oh, fuck. Yes. Yes, so fucking hot. Yes." Dal pushed back, rocking hard between Dillon's hand and his tongue.

Dillon curled his hand up, cupping Dal's balls, letting the motion of Dal's hand as he stroked himself push those balls right back into Dillon's hand. He pointed his tongue, pushed it in deep the next time Dal rocked back. The ties from the corset slid against his face, and he shuddered.

"Want you to fuck me. Hard and deep enough that I feel it for days."

His whole body pushed forward at Dal's words. "Oh, yeah, baby. That's the plan." He tongue fucked Dal a moment longer and then let go of the sweet balls, tugging the rings as he pulled his hand away. He held it out, palm up in front of Dal. "Lube."

"Mmmhmm." Dal chuckled, the sound all sex and pleasure and amusement. Then the slick tube was pushed into his hand. "What else is in here?"

"You want me to spoil the surprise?" He lubed up two fingers, and then watched them disappear into Dal's body as he pushed them into the tight, grasping heat.

"No. No, I fucking love surprises. They turn me on." Dal's head dropped and he started riding Dillon's touch, ass tight as a fist, body fucking demanding.

He loved that. Fucking loved it. Much as he might order people around as naturally as breathing, he wanted to be met head on by an equal.

"Glove," he muttered, tossing the tube onto the bed and reaching his hand out again.

"Say please."

He pushed his fingers deep, twisting them to find Dal's gland. He hit it and then hit it again, hard. Dal rippled, skin flushing dark, the white corset standing out. Oh, fuck. He'd never seen anything like it. Never wanted to fuck anyone as

Secrets, Skin and Leather

badly as he wanted to fuck Dal. "Please," he ground out, his need taking the lead.

"Yes." The condom was handed back, Dal panting now, ass squeezing Dillon's fingers rhythmically.

"Wait for me, baby." He tore the package open with his teeth, not willing to take his fingers out of Dal's ass yet. Besides, they were slick and wouldn't have been much help.

He got the condom on and only then pulled his fingers away.

"Come on. Come on, show me what you got. I need." That sweet hole was pink and slick and needed to be stretched and spread by his cock.

He slid his hands over Dal's hips, bringing them back as he lined his cock up with that hot little hole. He didn't plunge in, not this time. No, instead he pushed slowly, watching as the skin stretched around his prick, as it seemed to swallow the head of his cock right up.

A deep, raw sound filled the air, something no one on earth would believe could come from Scott Daly's lips.

"Fuck, yes." He kept pushing, not stopping until his hips were flush with Dal's ass, his cock deep inside Dal's body. "Ready, baby? Ready for me to fuck you good and hard?"

Dal looked over one shoulder, blue eyes clear as crystal, the hottest fucking thing Dillon'd seen in years. "You know it."

"Good."

He leaned in and took a kiss, hard and sure, tongue pushing into Dal's mouth before sliding over his lips. Then Dillon pulled back, pulled almost out, and looked down as he pushed back in again, his cock disappear into the tightest little ass he'd had in forever. The corset accented the view, the leather ties sliding against his prick, his hips, as well as Dal's ass.

Oh, fuck.

Groaning, he picked up the pace.

Dal was braced against the end table, thighs tight where Dillon slapped against them. Things passed through his mind -- reddening that pretty ass, seeing it filled and making the man dance for him, walk for him. Sweet fuck.

He slid his hand up along to the top edge of the corset and then followed it around to the front of Dal's body. His fingers slid up and found one of Dal's nipples, already hard and begging for his touch. He pinched it, timing the touch with the slam of his cock across Dal's gland.

That earned him a sharp scream, Dal's head thrown back as those hips pistoned back toward him. "Yes. Yes. Fuck."

He wasn't going to last long, not with the tight eagerness of Dal's ass around his cock, not with the scents that grew strong between them, and not with those sounds filling the air. Dal was the whole package. Just what he needed.

He doubled his efforts on Dal's nipples, fucked Dal harder. "Come for me, baby. Show me what you've got."

"Uh-huh. Uh-huh. Right. Fucking. There." Dal gripped him, shaking hard as the tight muscles rippled around his prick.

Secrets, Skin and Leather

"Yes." The word hissed from him as his climax built, gathered in his balls. He managed to hold on for a few more strokes, just pushing into Dal like all the secrets of the universe could be found inside him.

They stood there together, panting, Dal shaking under him, muscles rippling. He let his head rest on Dal's shoulder, his arm wrapping around Dal's waist, the feeling of leather against his sweaty skin wonderful. He pressed a kiss to Dal's back.

That had been better than he'd imagined, and he had quite the imagination.

"Tell me I have time for a shower before we have to meet up with all those assholes."

Dillon chuckled. "You have time for a shower." He moaned as he slipped from Dal's body. "And all those assholes left at the crack of dawn this morning."

"What? Why?" Dal stood, legs just a little shaky.

He turned Dal in his arms, looked into the blue eyes. "Because they weren't invited for the fuck-Dal-raw portion of the conference."

"Oh." One eyebrow went up, lips quirking in a wicked, impish smile. "I didn't see that on the schedule. I should have looked harder."

"I wasn't sure you'd stay if I included it," he admitted. Besides, he'd wanted a surprise seduction.

"I almost left the first night. It would have been wise."

Oh, no. No thinking. "It would have been

boring. Scott Daly would have done it." He slid his hands up over Dal's stomach, fingers teasing the pretty nipples as he reached them. "Dal needed to stay."

"Mmm..." Dal's eyes went half closed, lips parting. "Scott Daly is worth a good amount of money to his clients."

"For the next two days, Scott Daly is otherwise engaged. Where did you put the clamps?" He pinched one nipple and leaned forward to lick at the other.

"Under the pillow for the kinkfairy to find." Oh, listen to that husky laugh.

"The kinkfairy?" He chuckled, lying back on the bed to reach under the pillow. Dal stood between his legs, looking ravished and ravishing. Dillon's cock twitched. Hard.

"Mmm. Nice recovery time." Dal leaned forward, hands spreading out over his hips, thumbs nudging his balls.

"I'm inspired." His fingers hit something small and hard and he curled them around the clamps, drawing them out from under the pillow. Fuck, Dal was gorgeous, wearing his corset and nothing else, looking more than a little debauched.

"You didn't spend all night jacking yourself off." Those hands circled his cock, moving slow and easy, tight little ass swaying side-to-side.

He moaned a little, hips pushing into Dal's fingers. "Oh, to have been a fly on the wall..."

"You like to watch?" Fuck, those hands knew exactly how to touch, how hard, how fast.

Secrets, Skin and Leather

"A sexy thing like you? Fuck, yes, I like to watch." His voice had gone all rough and needy, and he couldn't stop his hips, couldn't do anything but let Dal have control.

"Mmm. What do you like best?" Dal hummed, eyes watching him, tongue wetting those pretty lips.

"Best? Me?" It wasn't a question he'd ever really asked himself. He wanted something, he took it, had it. His eyes half closed as he watched Dal working him, his body moving to Dal's rhythm.

"Yes. Best. As in, when you jack yourself off and you've got beautiful man willing to do anything behind your eyelids, what do you pick?"

"And are you going to perform my fantasy if I share it?" he asked, fingers curling around the clamps in his hand.

"Mmm... isn't that a luscious thought? Being in your fantasy. Tell me."

If only Dal knew he'd been the star of many a fantasy since that first night Dillon'd seen the man. "Now who's being bossy?" he asked, gasping as Dal's thumb pressed into his slit.

"Mmm... I'm being demanding. Bossy is completely different."

He chuckled, or at least tried to; the sound was rather twisted by another moan. He cleared his throat. "My fantasy boy wears a white corset. Done up tight enough he can barely breathe. It shapes his waist, shows off the flat tummy."

Dal hummed softly, leaned down to lick his

belly, the tip of his cock. "So far, so good. Keep going."

The nipple clamps bit into his palm as he clenched his hand harder, trying to concentrate on his words. It wasn't easy. Not with Dal touching and licking. "He... he's wearing a cock ring. It's tight. Around his balls, holding them tightly together and sepa...separated from his cock. He's hard. Are you hard, Dal?"

"Mmmhmm." Dal spread his thighs wider, hands cupping his ass, squeezing, pulling him up toward that mouth.

"Oh, yes," he murmured, ass flexing in Dal's hands. "Your mouth, please."

"Keep talking." Dal's lips rewarded him, dropping down over his cock, tongue moving and stroking, perfect against his skin.

Christ, Dal didn't ask for much, did he? Just coherence as his mouth did... oh, that....

"Ass full," he managed.

"Mmmhmm." Oh. Humming. Yes. Yes.

The sounds vibrated through him, making him shudder. "These on your nipples," he whispered, opening his hand and offering over the clamps.

One hand took the clamps, dragged the chain over his chest, down his belly, making him jerk and hum as the toy caught the hairs on his chest.

"They're quite tight," he told Dal, head moving back and forth on the bed. Christ, he felt incredible. Dal was something else. Dal's thumbs stroked his hole, stretched him just a little, pushed against him. "Fuck. Fuck." His hands grabbed onto the sheets, holding on tight. In his fantasies he never had to tell his lover what to do. Oh, he often did, but he didn't *have* to. "Dal. Yes."

Dal sucked and hummed, head beginning to bob, thumbs pressing in, spreading him.

Christ.

Damn.

His hips arched up off the bed, trying to push into Dal's mouth, to ride those fingers, but Dal had control, set the pace, set the rhythm. And, fuck, it was good. Dal took him in deep, swallowed around the tip of his cock, then pulled back, tongue teasing.

"Tease," he whispered, body just thrumming, balls aching.

"No. I put out." Dal kissed the tip of his cock, then sucked him right back in. His chuckle wound up being a groan, his body bucking, pushing his cock deeper.

"Put on the clamps." The words sounded more like a plea than an order, but it was the best he could manage with his cock buried in Dal's mouth.

Dal shifted so he could see, fingers pulling on those tight nipples, first one, then the other, making them hard.

Dillon panted, trying to catch his breath, to focus. Sexy. Hot. Christ, just watching Dal made him throb. "Now. Do it."

One clamp got clipped on, the suction around his cock growing stronger, more fierce.

"Yes!" His hips started moving again, finding

a rhythm that slid him deep every couple of seconds. His eyes stayed glued to Dal's body.

The second clamp went on, then his cock sank base-deep, Dal near devouring him. He shouted, hips slamming up. His hand reached, fingers wrapping in the short hair on Dal's head as he came, the heat pouring from him and down Dal's throat. Dal swallowed him down, throat working around him, lips and tongue cleaning him.

His hold on Dal's hair gentled, turned into petting. Fuck. He was... melted. Melted by a pretty, sexy man.

"Mmm..." Dal nuzzled his belly, lips hot and soft.

"Come up here," he ordered, wanting to taste himself in Dal's mouth.

"Bossy." Dal chuckled, tongue dragging up along his belly.

He chuckled, thumb sliding along Dal's cheek. "Assertive."

Dal turned his head, lips wrapping around Dillon's thumb. Dillon groaned, and he reached beneath Dal with his free hand, tugging on the chain. That mouth popped off his thumb, Dal crawling up along his body, lips swollen and parted. He slid his hand behind Dal's neck, and brought their mouths together. He could taste himself on Dal, sharp and salty.

His fingers slid, finding one of Dal's nipples, tracing where the clamp bit down on it. Dal hummed into his lips, little bit of flesh heated and hard for him. He slid his hand around and around the areole, and then, flicked his fingers across the clamp, watching Dal's face. Those eyes went wide, Dal jerking, thrusting against him with a husky cry.

"Hmm... you like that." He chuckled and flicked again. "You like it a lot." Christ, Dal was pure sex.

"I've had them on a few times. My nipples are sensitive now. Burned against my shirt."

"I want a meeting next week. A big one. Lots of people. You with your sensitive nipples, your ass full, those pretty little rings... Sitting there all prim and proper, but I'll know. I'll know every movement burns in your nipples and jolts the plug in your ass." God, the things he could do to Dal.

Dal chuckled against his lips. "I won't let you know, won't let you touch."

"Oh, I'll know. And you'll know what I want to do to you, you'll feel my touch in your mind." He slid his leg between Dal's, pushing up to rub against Dal's perineum.

Dal rubbed right back, the rings hot and smooth against his leg. "You're so sure I'd show."

"You'd show." He wriggled one of the nipple clamps, pushing harder with his leg. "You'll show."

"Will... Oh. Oh, fuck. Will I?" Dal started riding, hips rolling.

"You will." He rolled Dal suddenly, taking a long, hard kiss as he ground his knee against Dal's perineum. Dal arched up into him, fingers digging into his shoulders and holding on.

Breaking the kiss, he swiped his tongue across Dal's lips before bending to lick at one clamped nipple. Then he blew on it before nipping the skin just beneath it. Dal groaned, hands reaching up, wrapping around the headboard. He looked down at Dal, all stretched out for him and felt his prick try to struggle back to life. He laughed. Not this time, but he that didn't mean he couldn't play with this sexy body, that he couldn't make Dal just sing for him.

"You like cuffs?" he asked, hands sliding up along Dal's arms, wrapping around his hands and squeezing them.

"With the right playmates. I'll do anything with the right person."

"Anything? That sounds just about perfect, baby." He wanted to hear more about anything.

"You call all the men you seduce 'baby'?"

Dillon thought about it, and then shook his head. "There's only one other person I've ever called baby." Then he slid his hands back along Dal's arms, stroking across the shaved pits, hard enough not to tickle.

"Mmm... feels good." Dal arched, muscles going tight.

He loved how fucking sensual the man was. Loved that the strength and passion was a match for his own. He licked at Dal's pit, fingers sliding to catch the chain and tug on their way down to stroke the leather of the corset. Dal just groaned and nodded, body moving under his touch like the man was dancing.

While it would have been fun to have gotten it up again and fucked Dal's sweet ass again, there was something to be said for this -- for being able to take his time and watch and drive Dal right out of his mind. His fingers slid over the leather, measured Dal's waist in the tight cincher. That pretty prick curled up, the tip dark, dark red against the background of white. He flicked at it with his thumb. Dal jerked, cock bobbing, slapping the leather. It left a tiny wet spot behind and he leaned down, licked it away. Leather and salt mingled together in his mouth, and he moaned. He dragged his tongue along the edge of the corset, filling himself with the taste of leather and skin, the scents mingled together into an addictive bouquet.

"Tell me where you saw me. I had to have been out to play..."

"Are you sure?" Dillon asked. He licked his way along the hollow by Dal's hip, then nipped at the bone, a sharp little bite.

"Oh!" That sound was delicious, necessary. Hungry. He nodded, letting his cheek rub against Dal's prick. Christ, he wanted more of Dal's noises -- each one inspired him to press for the next.

He spread Dal's legs, tongue moving to the warm, smooth sacs. He frowned, the skin under the black curls wrong. Dark. "What's this?" he asked, pulling back a little, hands moving to try to push the curls away.

"Hmm?" Dal rolled up on his elbows, looking down. "Ink."

He drew his breath in on a gasp, heat going through him. Dal had mentioned surprises of his own. He looked up at Dal, grinning. "I'm shaving you."

Dal shook his head. "Now, now. Scott isn't shaved."

"You're not Scott here, baby. Here you're m- Dal." Mine. Where had that come from? "I want to see the ink."

"People in Hell want ice water." Look at those eyes laugh.

"Yes, I believe you've mentioned that before." He bent and nipped at the top of Dal's thigh, just where it met his groin. "Are you denying me?"

"You going to convince me I shouldn't?" Challenging bastard.

He sat back on his haunches between Dal's legs, let his hands run lightly along the lightly muscled thighs. "Denying can work both ways."

Dal shivered, muscles shifting. "You can always just imagine what it looks like..."

"I could. Would you tell me if I guessed right?" He slid one hand behind Dal's balls, tugged on one ring, but not the other.

"Mmm... mm-hmmm..." Dal's eyes drifted closed, legs spreading wider.

Chuckling, he slid his little finger through both rings, which just lightly jostled them. He bent and breathed on Dal's balls, letting his finger tug just a touch as he tried to guess what would be important enough to Dal to ink permanently upon his skin, but that he would desire to keep hidden.

Secrets, Skin and Leather

"A heart with 'mom' in it," he teased.

"Not even close." Dal chuckled, moaned, balls wrinkling and drawing up tight.

"Now that's either true, or you're trying to throw me off the scent." He nipped at one of Dal's balls, lips covering his teeth.

"No hearts. No names." Dal's knees drew up.

He took one of Dal's balls into his mouth and sucked, before letting it go, fingers toying again with the rings. "No, you're more likely to have Japanese characters. For strength or pleasure or passion."

Dal grinned. "Maybe."

Damn, Dal looked good happy. "You see? I know you more than you think." He rubbed his fingers against Dal's hole.

Dal laughed and winked. "Maybe not."

"Oh! Tease!" He pushed a second finger in along with the first and bent to take the head of Dal's prick into his mouth. The tip was leaking salt-bitter liquid that filled his mouth.

"Oh..." Dal arched, going still for a moment. He kept sucking, tongue swirling around the tip, tapping the slit as his fingers hit Dal's gland. "Right there. Fuck. Fuck. Right there."

He hummed, staying right where he was, just the head of Dal's cock in his mouth, tongue working it hard, fingers pushing against Dal's gland again and again. He could see the muscles of Dal's belly jumping beneath the leather corset, and further up the red, pinched nipples in their clamps, even higher Dal's fingers wrapped around the bedpost. Fucking gorgeous.

"I need to come. Fuck, it's good. Right fucking here. So good."

He pulled off, looked up into Dal's face. "You need permission?" As he asked, he pegged Dal's gland hard.

Dal laughed, eyes just sparkling. "Fuck, no. I like the anticipation, the ache."

"You like playing. Feeling. Fucking."

He hummed again and then took Dal in, all the way in. When the long prick hit the back of his throat, he swallowed around it. Dal started bucking, fucking his throat in short, sharp motions. He matched the rhythm, fingers pushing to hit Dal's gland over and over, while he reached up to grab the thin chain that connected the nipple clamps.

That's all it took, Dal's cock throbbing weakly in his mouth, the salt and bitter flooding him. He hummed, swallowing quickly, greedy for every last drop. He slowly pulled off Dal's prick, sucking hard as he did so until it popped out of his mouth. Then he licked it carefully, cleaning the hot, silky flesh as his fingers slid out of Dal's body. Dal just barely moved, melted and mostly asleep, slumped into the sheets.

"The clamps need to come off, baby," he murmured, fingers sliding up along the pretty corset. "You ready?" It was going to hurt pretty good.

"Mhph." He'd take that as a yes. Maybe.

He moved up so he was lying next to Dal, resting his weight on his side and one arm. His free hand rubbed Dal's belly for a moment and

Secrets, Skin and Leather

then back up to circle on nipple and then the other, drawing it out. For himself anyway. Chuckling, he grabbed one of the clamps and opened it, releasing Dal's nipple. He got a soft cry, Dal twisting and frowning, but those eyes didn't open.

"That tired or that used to it?" he asked, fingers sliding on the hard, red nipple, rubbing it as the blood rushed back into the flesh. Bending, he sucked it into his mouth, licked it gently as he reached and took off the other clamp.

"I. Oh. Oh, fuck. Ow. Just… Damn. Wore out. Haven't slept. Been thinking."

"Shh. Shh. I've got you," he murmured. He licked again, fingers rubbing the second nipple. "Thinking? I thought you were busy playing all night?"

"Uh-huh. Playing. Needing. Wondering who knew."

"Did you think it might be me?" He'd kept his cool, but he'd found himself eating Dal with his eyes more than once during the last two days.

"I… Once. Maybe. I don't know."

"Only maybe?" He pouted and then chuckled at himself, leaving a kiss on Dal's lips. "Do you want this off?" he asked, fingers sliding on the corset. It looked lovely, but Dal would be more comfortable when he woke if he wasn't wearing it. And Dillon was all about Dal being comfortable.

"Mmm. Please. Please."

"Okay, baby. You have to roll over." He encouraged Dal to roll over onto his stomach.

"Oh, fuck, I'd forgotten how good you looked from behind."

He slid his fingers over Dal's ass, the perfect little ass that had gone straight to his cock, the first time he'd seen it.

Dal spread, just purring. "Are you staying?"

"Yes." He let his fingers slide along the insides of Dal's thighs, teased his crack and then ran his fingers over that fine, fine ass again. He couldn't resist feeling Dal up in the corset one last time, the leather cooler than Dal's skin but still warm. He kept going when he hit skin, rubbing Dal's shoulders, before sliding his hands back down again.

He started working the first set of ties open. Dal just purred, melted and quiet and so fucking sexy for him. He took his time, letting his hands wander, his body slide against the smooth warmth of Dal's. He finally had all the ties undone and he slid his hands beneath the bottom of the corset, forcing the ties to loosen, to spread and release Dal from the tight hold.

Dal took a deep breath and stretched, that beautiful, tight ass wiggling.

"Feel good?" He pulled the corset open wider, hands massaging Dal's back.

"You do. So good."

Dillon hummed. It hadn't been what he'd meant, but he would take it. He would definitely take it.

He opened the corset right up, letting the ties pull right off one side, and then rolled Dal over onto his back again, tossing the corset on the floor. He let his touch continue, fingers massaging, working the skin, smoothing out the marks the tight leather had left. That Dal trusted him enough to simply float and rest said so much. He let his hands wander, exploring all of Dal, all that fine skin, before finally settling in next to him, curling up close. A flick of his wrist pulled the comforter over them.

"Rest," he murmured. "We can play more later."

"Mmmhmm." Dal pushed right in, the happy little sound just vibrating through him.

Dillon let his eyes close, his arms full of Dal's warmth.

He pushed away the thought that he could get used to this. He had two days. He would live in the moment and enjoy them.

Enjoy Dal.

Chapter Two

Dal stretched, little bits and pieces aching and stretching like he'd been playing hard the night before.

Morning before?

Something.

He floated and shifted, not waking up until his leg brushed up against somebody else's leg.

Oh, fuck him raw.

His eyes flew open and he just stared.

Dillon.

Fuck him.

The man looked softer in sleep, kind of at peace. The short hair was tousled, a satisfied half-smile on Dillon's lips. He was also utterly naked -- definitely not what he would have expected from the arrogant prick in the three-piece suit he knew in the boardroom.

"Mmm." Pretty. Pretty, pretty. Dal leaned over, lips brushing one pink, sweet nipple.

Dillon groaned and shifted, hand sliding over Dal's hip as Dillon's flesh hardened under his tongue, seemed to reach up toward his tongue. He closed his eyes, licking and sucking gently, just feeling and floating, nice and easy. Not thinking.

The hand on his hip slid up along his side, the touch firm and warm. "Dal... fuck, that's a nice way to wake up."

"Mmmhmm." Nice voice, husky. Happy. Warm.

Dillon arched, pushing that nipple into his mouth. One leg slid over his, moving slowly to hook around his knee and tug him closer. Dal cuddled in, humming nice and low, just snuggling into that heat.

"I should have put a plug in you before we dozed off." Dillon's hand slid down to his ass, squeezed firmly.

Oh. Yummy. "Don't have any plugs here, man."

Dillon chuckled, the sound husky. "Oh, I think that drawer of goodies might have one or two. I did mention the staff had stocked the place while you were at breakfast, didn't I?" He could feel Dillon's cock now, pushing against his hip.

"I think so?" He hadn't been paying attention.

Dillon chuckled, the sound matching the movements of the wide chest he rested on. "You were a bit... busy."

"Mmmhmm." He couldn't believe this. That he was here. Like this. "Where did you see me?"

"You don't believe that I saw through that straight-laced suit and prim attitude and knew?" Dillon's fingers slid along his spine, right down to the top of his ass, where they slid and circled.

"Not a chance. You never even noticed me in the suit."

"Yes, I did. I thought you were the world's biggest prude in a world of big prudes." He could hear the laughter in Dillon's voice. "And then I went to the Golden Scabbard for a drink and found out that I could still be oh so very wrong."

"Oh, God." Dal's cheeks heated. God, he thought that was far enough away from home. "You were slumming."

"I wasn't the only one." Dillon shrugged. "Sometimes... well, you know." Dillon's hips pushed up, sliding the long, hard cock along his skin.

"I know." He never thought anyone would recognize him. Ever.

Dillon's fingers slid down along his crack, straight to his hole. "I wanted you the second I saw you."

"Yeah? I wouldn't have been on stage there. Wouldn't have been with Rouge or Jim. I'd have been dancing."

"On *stage*." Dillon made a sound that might have been a purr, might have been a whimper, and Dillon's finger pushed into him. "You were dancing. I want to see the other."

He hummed, jonesing on the stretch. "I like to play. Like to take chances." He loved it.

"Then let's play. Lean over and pull the first thing you touch out of the bottom drawer." Oh, there was seduction in that voice, Dillon inviting him to have fun, to let go.

He looked into those eyes, trying to decide if this was real. If this was actually happening. If he could trust Dillon as far as he could throw the man. Then he reached down and picked, without even so much as feeling what he grabbed. Might as well be hung for a sheep as well as a lamb.

Secrets, Skin and Leather

"Oh, Dal, I do like the way your luck runs." Dillon took the toy from him and held it out for him to see. It was long and thin, with a round ball at one end, a wire coming out from the back of the ball. A penis wand. One that did something.

Vibrated or sparked or *something*.

His eyes popped open. "That looks terrifying." Sexy as fuck, but terrifying.

Dillon laughed. "Do you trust me, Dal? Will you let me put it in you? I promise it'll be fun. Arousing. Exciting. And you won't be able to come until I take it out."

"You going to tell me what it does?" Hell, yes. He'd let.

Dillon slid the wand against his neck, the metal cold but quickly warming on his skin. "I thought you liked surprises?"

Dal nodded. They turned him on. The unknown. The unexpected. The whole fucking thing.

"Then you'll just have to wait and see what it does." Dillon's eyes shone, heat and arousal making them dark. "Let's make this really interesting. I'll pull something out as well."

"Mmm." Dillon would have to lean over him, bring that fine body close enough to bite.

Sure enough, Dillon rolled against him, pushing him to his back and leaning all over him as Dillon reached into the drawer. He grabbed hold of one nipple with his teeth, biting, marking.

Dillon gasped and jerked against him. "Dal...

Damn." Oh, Dillon's voice was husky, sexy and wanton.

"Uh-huh." He bit again, moaning low. Damn. Possibly also fuck.

Dillon grabbed something and pushed against him, cock hot and hard between them, chest pressing down against his mouth. Demanding man. Dal went with it, biting and marking, fingers digging into the man's ass. Yeah. C'mere. Fuck.

"Christ, you make me need, Dal." Whatever Dillon had pulled out of the drawer was dropped on the bed beside them, Dillon lining their cocks up and rubbing them together, grinding down against him. He was going to chafe or die of permanent orgasms or something. What a way to go.

He arched up, meeting each thrust, each motion. Dillon shifted again, and suddenly his cock was rubbing along Dillon's crack.

"You want it?" Dillon asked him.

"Do you?" He loved fucking. Loved feeling. Loved the whole fucking thing.

Dillon nodded. "I want to feel you inside me. Get a taste of the whole package." Dillon reached again, handed him the tube of lube and a condom.

"Works for me." He could handle that. He handed the lube back over and took the condom. "Let me watch you slick yourself up."

"Oh, you're a naughty boy."

Dillon gave him a hard kiss and then rose up onto his knees. The hard body towered over him,

Secrets, Skin and Leather

Dillon spreading lube on his fingers and then reaching back. It arched the man's back, pushing the hard cock and tight, high balls toward him. Oh, the man was fucking fine. Dal worked the condom open, started stroking it on while his other hand reached for that heavy, heated column of flesh.

Dillon groaned as he touched it, the skin like silk against his fingers, so damned soft over a core like steel. More groans filled the air as Dillon danced for him, pushing against his own hand and riding back on long fingers.

His cock felt like steel, his balls drawing up tight. "Fucking fine, Dillon."

Oh, that made the man preen, and the next thing he knew, Dillon was reaching back for his cock, guiding it to a hot, tight little hole. "Not so bad yourself, Dal." And then Dillon pushed down onto his cock.

"Fuck, yes." Dal arched and thrust, eyes rolling as that hot sheath squeezed his prick tight.

Dillon's hands landed on either side of his head, and his cock was squeezed even tighter and then slowly released as Dillon pulled up and almost all the way off.

"Yeah. Fuck. Yes." Dillon nodded and grinned and then started to ride, up and down on his prick like a pro.

The top of his head was going to come right off, just pop off, but, fuck, it would be worth it. It would. Shit.

Dillon's mouth dropped over his, tongue

pushing into his mouth as their bodies started to slam together. His fingers dug into Dillon's hips, tugging, pulling, adding his strength to Dillon's. Yeah. Yeah, like that.

"I like your strength," muttered Dillon. "Hate weakness." Dillon started rising and falling faster, harder, skin breaking out with sweat.

"Uh-huh. Keep moving." He braced his heels against the mattress and thrust up harder, burning, inside and out.

"Fuck, yes." Dillon's elbows locked, his movements matching Dal's, the noise of their bodies slapping together louder than his breath and the sound of his heart pounding.

Oh, shit. Soon. It was so fucking hot. Soon.

Dillon shifting and shouted, eyes going wide. "Fuck! Right there!" The man's motions became almost frantic, hand sliding to grab at his cock.

"Yeah. Yeah. Right. There. Fuck." He grunted, teeth sinking into his bottom lip.

Dillon's tongue swiped at his teeth, his lip, and the man just bounced on him. Dal's eyes suddenly went wide, Dillon's ass squeezing him tight as heat spurted between them. Oh, now. That was just fucking amazing. It didn't take too long for him to follow, for his belly to go tight and his balls to draw up as he shot. Dillon collapsed onto him, still holding his cock in tight heat, breath warming his neck as the man panted.

"Nice," grunted Dillon.

"Better than." Way better than nice. Fuck.

Dillon nodded and then groaned, pulling off him and shifting to lie next to him. Another grunt and Dillon arched up, reaching beneath himself and laughing as he pulled a pair of cuffs from where they'd been tossed on the bed.

"We were going to play."

"We were?" Fuck, the man could recover from the post-fucking blinkies quick.

"Before you jumped me, yeah." He was given a wink, Dillon still chuckling, rolling to his side and sort of wrapping around him.

"You were on top. You jumped me."

Dillon laughed. "I believe it was your teeth that started this." Dillon's voice lowered. "Dragging over my skin, biting my nipple..." One of Dillon's fingers found Dal's nipple and let the nail scrape over it.

"Mmm... You put it in my mouth..." Oh. Burned. Good.

Dillon's lips twitched. "Oh, I did, did I? And I suppose I put your cock in my ass as well." This time Dillon grabbed his nipple and tweaked it. Then Dillon laughed, the sound bright and sexy. "Actually, I did, didn't I?"

"You did. Smartass." He leaned over, took himself a nice, hard kiss.

That stopped Dillon's laughter, the man's mouth opening for him, letting him lead, letting him dominate the kiss and make it what he wanted it to be. A low moan filled him, Dillon's hand flattening against his chest. He hummed, the kiss more relaxed and easy, exploratory. Lazy.

Fucking sweet.

They shifted together, legs tangling, bodies

pressing warmly together as each kiss was broken by slow, deep breaths before sliding into another and into another. Dillon's hands weren't still, mapping his body like the man was memorizing it. His skin was just singing, muscles shifting and sliding as he responded to Dillon's touch.

"So sensual. So sexy. All hidden away so no one can see..." Dillon's eyes met his as one of the handcuffs closed around his wrist.

Dal blinked, surprised. Shit. He hadn't been paying attention. "Sneaky."

Dillon grinned, stretching Dal's arm up to the headboard and attaching the other cuff to it. "Just trying to make sure I deliver on the surprise portion of this little adventure." He tugged, feeling the pull, the rush, the faint anxiety that was so fucking *hot*. Dillon laughed softly and nipped at his collarbone. "You're caught. Mine." Warm and wet, Dillon's tongue dragged across Dal's chest to his left nipple, where it teased him with light, barely there touches.

"Yours? You... Oh. Oh, that's good. You don't know me yet." Fuck, that felt nice.

"Right here, right now, you're mine." Dillon popped his head up, grinning at him. "You're caught in my snare, Dal." Dillon's hand slid from where his wrist was cuffed to the bed on down to his hip. "Now what should I do with you?"

"What do you want to do with me? What turns you on?"

"I want to do everything." Dillon's voice was like a purr. "Play with every toy, fuck you six ways to Sunday, make you scream with pleasure." Dillon reached over and pulled up the penis wand. "I want to start with this."

"That's one Hell of a way to start." He spread his legs, toes curling a little in anticipation.

"You chose it," Dillon reminded him with a wink. Dillon stopped suddenly, fingers sliding across his belly. "Would you like another corset first?"

"I'm a little tied up." Another? Goddamn. "How many are there?"

"I would put you in it, of course." Dillon stood and went over to the dresser, opening the bottom drawer. "I chose several especially for you."

A deep blood-red corset was pulled from the drawer, the lacing black. "This one does up in front."

Dillon brought it over, showed it to him. It was leather, just like the white one, but worked until it was butter-soft. It was larger than the other one as well -- it looked like it would go from just below his nipples all the way down over his hips.

"It's beautiful..." He arched, hands trying to reach for it, trying to touch. Dillon slid it over his arm, teasing his fingers with it before dragging it down and letting it touch his face, his chest, his cock.

"You're going to look amazing in it." Dillon's voice was husky, his eyes gone dark and hot.

"You should see me with my eyes done, my nipples rouged." He looked otherworldly.

Sexual.

Dillon licked his lips. "That's almost enticing enough to get me to let you out of the cuffs..." The corset was wrapped around his cock, Dillon jacking him off with it.

"Mmm. We... Oh. We have time." Damn. Almost slick. Almost. God.

"You like that, Dal? It's going to smell of you while you wear it. Smell like your need." Dal's hand squeezed, drops of pre-come leaking from him and wetting the soft leather.

"Don't want to stain it... Oh, God. Fuck. Hot. It's so fucking soft."

"If we ruin it, I'll buy you a new one." Dillon stopped, though, sliding the corset up over his belly, and bending to lick at the tip of his prick, tongue hot, pushing against his slit. The sounds he was making were obscene, wanton, perverse. Loud.

The corset slid up over him, rubbed against his nipples as the head of his cock was taken into Dillon's mouth. So hot, Dillon's suction strong, and that tongue danced over his head, tapped against his slit. Shit. Shit, that was. Damn. And it was going to get worse. Sharp. Sensitive as fuck. The corset rubbed and rubbed against his nipples, Dillon pinching them through it. And Dillon's tongue played and swirled over his head, pushed into his slit. It was obvious Dillon was in no hurry to make him come, only wanting to overload him with sensation.

Fucking maddening. Really. Goddamn. His... shit. His own babble drove him crazy, then he sort of settled into it, went from frantic to floating. Dillon seemed to know, humming, the suction easing a little and then disappearing altogether as his cock was released.

"Time to dress you up, beautiful." Dillon pushed a hand beneath Dal's back and arched him up off the bed, sliding the corset beneath him.

Warm. Fuck. Nice and warm. "Mmm... Pretty..."

"It shows your skin off," murmured Dillon, fingers beginning the long task of lacing up the ties. "I'm going to make it tight. Draw in your waist nice and small."

"Good. Love the way it feels, like having a lover hold me."

Dillon's fingers teased Dal's skin now and then as he worked the ties closed and then began the task of tightening the leather. "Take a breath and hold it as long as you can, baby."

Baby. The word made him ache a little, made him moan as he took a deep breath.

"Oh, yes, just like that." Dillon's finger slid across his lips, and then the corset began to tighten around him. Tighter and tighter Dillon drew it, until Dal could feel every inch of it trying to become a part of his skin. His heart pounded, head swimming as he held his breath. Oh, fuck. Yes. Sweet.

He didn't think it could go any tighter, but Dillon managed, drawing his waist in, the leather almost biting into his hips. Then Dillon used the ends of the leather ties to bind his cock and his balls. His breath whooshed out of him, his low cry echoing. Fuck, Dillon was good.

A low noise came from Dillon's throat, the man standing back and looking down at him. "Stunning." Reaching out, Dillon let a single finger slide the length of his prick. His entire body arched, just begging for Dillon's touch, for Dillon's caress.

"Shit, you're sexy, Dal." Dillon settled back on the bed between his legs, fingers moving and sliding, tracing the shape of his prick, the veins and bumps. The touches were sweet, but gentle, soft, barely enough. Dal soared, each and every nerve just singing, begging for more, for the touches to continue.

"So pretty." Dillon's fingers slid across the tip of his cock, played there, rubbing back and forth across his slit. His breath started panting in time with the touches, heart slamming in his chest. "Mmm... you're just about ready for the wand, aren't you?" Dillon squeezed the head of Dal's cock, finger pushing in.

His thighs went tight, head lifting from the mattress. "Fuck. Fuck, you'll drive me crazy." He'd fucking kill the man if Dillon stopped.

"Yeah? It's a good place to be." Dillon gave him a wink and then picked up the wand in one hand, the lube in the other, slowly slicking the metal up.

He couldn't help vibrating, just almost aching, almost burning, balls to bones. Dillon pressed some lube into his slit, eyes watching him as the cold slick was pushed into him. "That. That always feels weird. Always." His thighs were shaking, shuddering, nerves just jumping.

"Not as weird as it's going to." More lube was pushed into his slit, Dillon's finger lingering this time, sliding back and forth across the tip of his cock, making him insane. "You want it, Dal?"

"Fuck." He nodded, bit his bottom lip good and hard. Yeah. No. Shit, he didn't know.

Dillon growled a little, the sound hot and kind of distracting. The warm hand around his prick squeezed the head again, making his slit go round, and then the tip of the wand swirled around the head of his cock, teased the slit, pushed in just a touch and then came back out again. "So fucking pretty."

"Fuck. I... That's... I..." Okay. Breathe. No babbling. None.

"Yeah. Look at you." Dillon's voice was husky. "Gonna get serious about this now."

The wand teased the tip of his prick a moment longer, and then Dillon began to really, really slowly push it into him. His breath caught in his chest, eyes fastened on the sight of the rod sliding into him.

Into him.

Fuck.

Dillon didn't stop, just kept slowly filling him impossibly with the wand, the ball at the top getting closer and closer to the top of his cock. "That's it, baby. Take it in. Christ, you were made for this, weren't you?"

All he could do was nod, lips parted, heart just pounding in his chest.

"Yeah. Fucking amazing." Dillon kept pushing, kept filling until the little ball at the top was resting against his prick, the entire wand inside him. "Dal. Fuck. Oh, fuck, baby." Dillon's hands slid along his thighs, rubbing.

He just spread and spread, groaning as his head fell back. "Dillon."

"And I haven't even started it vibrating yet." Dillon's fingers slid over his balls, his prick, touching his skin and the dark leather of the ties that were wrapped around him. Then Dillon's finger touched the top of the ball, jostling it just a little.

"V...vibrating." Fuck. Shit, that was intense. Sharp. Fucking astounding.

"Yeah. Don't worry, baby, we'll start slow and work our way up." Dillon didn't wink or chuckle. The man looked serious as a heart attack and turned on as fuck. The ball was jostled again, and then Dillon flicked each of his nipples, almost making them echo the touch to his cock.

"Kiss me." Thoughts were chasing themselves around and around in his brain, just maddening.

"Bossy," murmured Dillon, but the man leaned over him, bringing their lips together. Dillon slowly lowered himself onto Dal, pressing against him, hotter where they weren't separated by the leather of the corset. It pressed his cock between them, making him even more aware of the rod inside him. He whimpered, the sound pushing into Dillon's mouth, hips rocking the slightest bit.

"You're so fucking hot for it," muttered Dillon, breaking the kiss only long enough to say the words before diving back into his mouth. One of Dillon's hands slid between them, fingers finding Dal's nipple and tweaking it. His own hands tugged against the chains, the sound loud as he pulled and tried to reach.

Dillon chuckled, the sound pushing against his lips, and then backed off, eyes glittering down at him. "It's about to get crazy."

"You think I'm ready for crazy?" His heart was trip-hammering.

"I think you've been looking for crazy all your life." Dillon's eyes held his, watching as Dillon fiddled with something out of sight, and suddenly the rod in his prick began vibrating.

"Oh. Oh, fuck." He scrambled back, the sensation unlike anything he could fucking understand.

"Shh. Shh. Just relax a little, Dal, or you're not going to make it up to high." Dillon's fingers slid along his cock, a gentle, warm counterpoint to the vibrations coming from inside it. They moved down and cupped his balls, squeezed them a little.

"I. Shit, I didn't expect. I mean. Fuck, it's intense."

"Incoherent looks good on you, baby," murmured Dillon, bending to gnaw at his nipple, teeth sharp and eager on his skin. The hand around his balls squeezed again and then drifted backward, sliding over the soft, sensitive skin behind them. The touch actually eased him a little, relaxed him, helped him to breathe. Dillon moaned a little. "Yeah, that's it. Go with it instead of fighting it."

Dillon's fingers crept right back to Dal's hole, teasing it as the vibrations ratcheted up just a touch higher. He twisted, stretching and arching, trying to make room inside him for all the sensations.

"Want me to fuck you while you're flying, baby?" Dillon's mouth licked up alongside his prick, nibbled at the bottom of the corset and then toothed his nipple.

"Uh-huh." Words were beyond him, really. He was all about grunts and clicks.

"Yeah, I want that, too."

The vibrations got more intense, stronger, and two of Dillon's fingers pushed right into his ass, slick and cool, warming quickly. His head tossed and he just went from ninety to nothing, entire focus on his need, on the way his nerves were firing. Dillon's fingers found his gland, working it as the man's mouth slid over his nipples, his neck, bit and licked and added just one more sensation to the many that were threatening to overwhelm him completely.

All of that, and he couldn't come. God.

Dillon was talking, grunting or something, Dal didn't know, could hear the low, sexy voice but not the words. It didn't matter, it was just one more thing. Then he was empty, but not for long. Soon the blunt, hard, hot head of Dillon's cock was pushing into him. Yes. Fuck, yes. Please. Everything inside him was screaming, every nerve just lit like fire.

Before Dillon slid home, the vibrations got even more intense, almost too much. Then Dillon slid home, cock pushing deep, hot and solid, real. Dal couldn't breathe, couldn't think, all he was was cock and ass and pure need. Dillon didn't leave him hanging in the wind, just started pounding into him, ramming that hard cock into his ass over and over until he was flying, so fucking high.

The sensations all twisted together, Dillon's heat and low sounds the only other things that were real. He started begging, pleading, the pleasure threatening to be too big, too much, too sharp. He could feel it sliding there, heading from overwhelmingly good to just overwhelming. Just before that happened, the wand was pulled out of him, the sudden absence of the vibrations amazing.

"Come," grunted Dillon, slamming into him.

The world went a pale grey, everything swirling as his brains shot out his cock. Dillon shouted, the sound following him into his floating, melted world.

It was Dillon's weight that first penetrated his fog. Heavy and warm and on top of him, holding him. He tried to move his hands, settled for snuggling in.

Dillon moaned softly, prick sliding out of him. "Oh, fuck, Dal. That was..." The man grunted and shifted a bit, hands sliding to undo the cuffs.

He nodded, he thought.

Maybe.

Or not.

God.

Dillon shifted again, tugging him into the long arms and nuzzling his neck. "I move we stay in bed and nap."

"Motion seconded."

"Passed." Dillon grunted and tugged him closer, one leg going over both of his. "Wildcat."

He just chuckled, cuddled in. Yeah. That was him. Wild.

Dillon's hand settled on his belly, hot through the corset, and the man's weight slowly grew heavy.

Goddamn. This was the best business conference in history.

And he still had another day.

Lucky him.

***

Dillon was still asleep.

He couldn't hear the rain on the trees and the sand and the roof of Dal's cabin. He couldn't feel time sliding through his fingers, moving inexorably to the time Dal had to get on the boat back to the mainland to catch his plane.

Nope.

All he could feel was Dal's body snuggled close to his, hot skin and cool PVC corset pressed against him. His cock throbbed. Damn, but Dal looked good in black.

Okay, so maybe he wasn't all that asleep.

His fingers started wandering, tracing the bottom of the corset just above Dal's perfect little ass. That sweet hole had been slicked and licked, touched and fucked, now it was plugged and full. It made him growl a little, his fingers sliding down along Dal's crack. He wondered what kind of reaction he'd get if he jostled the heavy plug...

Dal murmured, entire body rippling, ass shifting, body twisting toward and away from him. He chuckled, growing more awake by the second. Anyone who could sleep through Dal's body shifting against their own didn't deserve to enjoy the wildcat in bed. He gave the plug a good, hard jostle and a twist, pushing his hips into Dal's.

Dal's eyes popped open, the blue burning into his, shocked and hungry all at once.

Fuck, he loved that, the hunger and the surprise both. Even after two days of doing wonderful, perverse things to each other, Dal could look surprised that he was here, that he knew. It was delicious.

He bit at Dal's lower lip and jostled the plug again. Dal grunted, hips beginning to roll, moving between his body, his hand. So fucking sensual. And needy. He fucking loved it. He bit again and then turned it into a kiss, pushing his tongue into Dal's mouth. Dal met him head-on, the passion overwhelming and sure, Dal never shrinking away.

He rolled onto his back, tugging Dal with him. The weight of the man felt good, matched the passion and need that flowed between them.

And it gave him the perfect opportunity to slide his hands along Dal's back, the corset, and that sweet ass, which he grabbed in both hands, squeezing, knowing it would make the plug move again.

"Mmmhmm." Dal straddled him, balls soft and hot where they rubbed against him.

Groaning, he rocked his hips upward, sliding their cocks together.

"Oh, yeah," he murmured, squeezing Dal's cock again. Felt so good being done to as much as he was doing.

"So fucking hot." Dal groaned, nipping his lips.

He nodded, mouth chasing Dal's, wanting more than the nips, wanting full-on heat. There was a lurid bruise on Dal's collarbone, and he brought one of his hands up to press at it. His mark on the lovely, lovely skin. Dal's hips bucked. The cry pushed into his lips, Dal's cock sliding against his belly as the sound slid over his tongue. He'd been good, left the mark below where Dal's collar would be, but the temptation was huge to mark him further up.

Groaning, he slid his hands back to Dal's ass, grabbing it hard to keep them occupied. Dal chuckled, like the little ass knew what he was thinking. That ass wiggled, just rocking in his hands. He let his fingers slide and hit the plug again, reward or punishment -- it was all the same -- and leaned up, biting at Dal's bottom lip, pulling it into his mouth and sucking. He felt every inch of Dal's shudder, those long fingers tangling in his hair. He twisted the plug, biting down hard on Dal's lip. Every response from Dal sent a thrill through him, made him want another and then another, made him want each one to be more than the last.

"Fuck. More." Dal's eyes rolled, heart just pounding against him.

Grabbing the base of the plug, he tugged it out before jamming it back in again, slamming it home. "I'll give you more. I'll give you everything you can handle."

Those pale blue eyes stared at him, dazed and needy and shocked. "I'd like to see you try."

"Stick around, baby, and you will." He changed the angle of the plug, searching for Dal's gland. Dal's breath huffed out of him in a rush when he pegged it, those fingers in his hair tugging. He grinned, laughed, feeling on top of the fucking world. He pushed the plug past Dal's gland again, fingers of his free hand creeping between them so he could twist Dal's nipple. It was hard in his fingers, begging for it.

Hungry bastard. Taking everything he offered and asking for more.

He pushed up against Dal, their pricks sliding and rubbing. Such fucking heat and passion and all for him. He pushed the plug in harder, faster, watching the pleasure in Dal's eyes. "Gonna be hell, leaving this tomorrow."

"Uh-huh." Dal made it tempting to throw it all to the winds and just fuck until they both faded away.

"Got vacation time due?" he asked. And

damn. When was the last time he gave enough of a shit to make future plans? Not that that mattered right now, not with Dal's prick leaving his belly wet.

"I have a deal in London, then Tokyo. After that, I can schedule time." Dal bit his throat, moaning against his skin.

Groaning, he arched hard, offering more skin. "I have a country house..." Isolated, quiet. Well-stocked.

He got another bite, sharp and deep, marking him. "Where?"

A shudder went through him, his cock throbbing. Fuck, he wanted inside Dal. "Maine. On a private beach." He twisted the plug, pushed it in hard and then tugged it out.

"Oh..." Dal nodded, groaned against his neck. "Yes."

He grabbed Dal's hips and raised him a touch, getting his own prick out from between them and back to slide past Dal's balls and along his crack.

"Condom." The word was nearly barked out, but, fuck, he needed to sink into Dal's heat, needed it bad.

"Pushy." Dal stretched, reached, let him see that lean form, the black curls Dal still hadn't let him shave. His fingers found the little rings, pulling and tugging.

"Just want you, Dal." So fucking badly. His fingers teased his own prick as he played with the rings. "Don't tell me you don't want that sweet ass filled."

"I'd be lying if I did. I need you. Hard and

deep." The condom was handed over. "Now."

He nodded. "I know."

He held Dal's eyes as he tore open the condom and smoothed it over his cock. Dal was slick and stretched from sleeping with the plug in, and Dillon guided his prick to the needy little hole. "Ride me, Dal. Take it."

Dal grabbed the headboard, arching and pushing right down on his cock. Fuck. Fuck, hot. Tight. His. Fuck. Dal was so fucking sexy, rising up from his body like some sort of sex god. Lovely pale skin and dark corset. Fucking stunning. He slid his hand over Dal's hips, and then on up along the PVC.

"Gonna make sure you remember me," Dal said. He moved, danced on Dillon's cock, those amazing eyes staring down at him. Dillon doubted there was any danger he would be forgetting Dal anytime soon, but if the man wanted to give him a ride to remember, he wasn't going to say no.

His thumbs brushed across Dal's nipples, the pretty little bits of flesh dark and swollen from use. There were the prettiest bruises and marks scattered over the lean body, just decorating Dal. His marks, his bruises, put there by his hands and his mouth, his teeth. Moaning, he planted his feet on the mattress and bucked up, pushing into Dal's body, adding his strength to their joining.

"Yeah..." Dal arched, bouncing on his prick, fingers white-knuckled on the headboard.

He craned his neck up and managed to wrap his lips around one nipple, sucking and licking, biting. His hands pulled Dal's hips down.

"More. Shit. Come on, Dillon. So fucking close."

Growling a little, he grabbed Dal around the waist and flipped them, putting Dal on the bottom. Then he started pounding that sweet fucking ass, giving Dal everything he had. Dal wasn't the only one wanting to be remembered.

Dal shot hard, spunk spraying over his belly, Dillon's name ringing out. That sweet, most perfect ass squeezed tight around him, milking his cock, and Dillon's own cry joined Dal's as he shot hard. Groaning, panting, he lowered himself onto Dal, cock still sheathed in Dal's heat.

"So good. So fucking good." Dal nuzzled into Dillon's throat, lips parted on his skin.

He made a humming noise in reply, the sound turning into a groan of disappointment as he slid out of Dal's body. He got rid of the condom and rested his head on Dal's shoulder. "Definitely memorable."

"Good. I hate to be forgotten before I'm gone."

He chuckled. "Oh, there's no chance of that happening." Not one fucking chance. "Though I might need a reminder by the time you're back from -- was it Tokyo?"

"Mmmhmm. It was. Is... How can I get in touch with you, after Tokyo?"

Dillon thought about that. This was none of his secretary's business. He wasn't home enough to make giving that number out worth it. He gave Dal his private cell phone number. "Call that when you need me." And he had no doubt that Dal would call, that the need would rise in the man. And he'd more than proved he could give Dal exactly what was needed.

"I can do that." Dal took a long, slow deep kiss. "We've still got one day, though."

He opened wide, inviting Dal in for another kiss. "We do. If you're sure you don't want to spend it out on the beach." He kept a straight face, giving Dal his most earnest look.

"I'd burn if we fucked on the beach all day."

He laughed long and hard at that. "Yeah, and it would be a shame to burn or sandpaper this lovely skin." He let his fingers linger, loving the way skin became PVC and then PVC became skin again. "Only bruises and bite marks for you, baby."

"I'll keep that in mind."

He chuckled, fingers finding a bruise on Dal's collarbone and pressing into it. His stomach growled loudly and he chuckled. "I should call for breakfast. You want anything special?" He was thinking fruit with cream. He'd take that corset off and make Dal his table. He could already taste the cream with the salt of Dal's skin mixed in.

"Food. I'm starving." Dal smiled and stretched. "Although there should be coffee. Good, rich coffee."

"Yeah, I bet that's a wonderful taste on your lips." He went to the phone, admiring each move Dal made. His cock was at half mast again already, a testament to just how fucking sexy Dal was. He didn't think he'd come this much in the last six months.

"Mmm. I should probably bathe, too, huh?" The long legs spread, stretched, wanton bastard.

"It'll take a while for the food to get here. And I don't know if you noticed, but the showers here are enormous." More than big enough for two. He licked his lips and pressed 98 for the kitchen. He ordered scrambled eggs and bacon, toast, fresh fruit and cream. And a pot of dark roast coffee.

"I have noticed." Those pretty eyes shone at him over Dal's shoulder as the man stood. "I spent one night in there with a dildo and the nipple clamps."

He hung the phone up with a bang, his cock jerking at the words. "You are so wicked. I would like to have seen that. I'd ask for a show, but I'd rather help than watch."

That pert, tight ass just wiggled, showing off for him. "Promises, promises."

He groaned and started going through the drawer. "Did I arrange to have a paddle put in here?"

That ass would look amazing with a welt or two across it. And if there was no paddle, Dillon would find something else for them to play with. Dal laughed and hurried toward the bathroom. He couldn't find a paddle, but he did find a rubber glove with little rubber prickles on it. Oh, the things this could do to that pretty skin. Moaning at the thought, he grabbed the glove and hurried after Dal.

The water was running, Dal twisting and turning, trying to get himself out of the corset. Dillon chuckled, the sound husky. Damn, Dal made him want like no one ever had.

"You need a hand, baby? Maybe two?"

"Hell, yes. This thing's wrapped around me tighter than a fist."

He stepped up behind Dal, rubbing his cock along that perfect ass as his fingers slid along the corset, down to the knots.

He licked at Dal's neck. "You look stunning all trussed up. I'm going to have so much fun finding new corsets for you to wear."

"You'll have to see my collection some day. I have a black leather one with a crotch strap. One of white kidskin..."

Groaning, he bit down on Dal's skin as he worked the ties on the corset loose. "You'll have to bring them with you after Tokyo... along with your kohl and your rouge." He could remember how good Dal looked at the Scabbard that night, fully decked out. And maybe he had a collection of his own. Dal didn't need to know that yet, though. He spread the corset wide, watching as Dal's whole body seemed to take a deep breath.

"I can do that. Who knows what I'll find in Tokyo..." Dal wiggled, stretched.

He pulled the corset right off and let his hand slide on Dal's skin. So warm and smooth, just beautiful. He liked the idea of Dal buying things to wear with him in mind. He slid his cock along Dal's crack. "Let's get into the water," he murmured, pushing forward gently, encouraging

Dal toward the shower as his hand slid down over Dal's belly.

"Mmmhmm." Dal stepped forward, face lifted to the spray.

He stayed with Dal, fingers sliding on slick, wet skin now. "Soap," he muttered, eager to touch Dal all slicked up.

"Bossy." The bar was handed back, the soap round with heavy nubs, perfect for massaging, for rubbing.

"That's because I'm the boss," he pointed out. Okay, so he might not be the boss of Dal himself, but he was the boss of a shitload of people.

He soaped up both hands and then started running them over Dal's front, soapless hand gliding and the other one rubbing, using the bumps to best effect.

"Mmm..." Dal braced against the marble tile, hands pale against the black stone. "Yeah."

"You're just a hedonist, aren't you, Dal?" He chuckled, the sound almost a moan as it dragged out of him.

He spent time soaping up Dal's chest -- way more time than was needed, but it was good, this slick, gliding touch, the soap bumping along Dal's skin. He rubbed soap and fingers over Dal's nipples, sliding over them, and then crossing his hands to change things up, soap now on the left, just fingers on the right. He slid down over Dal's ribs and the sweet six-pack, skating over to rub Dal's hips, and then coming on back up again, all the way to the sharp collarbones.

"You make me feel good." Dal's head fell forward. "It's insane."

Dillon nibbled at Dal's neck, sucking the water right off the pale skin. "There's nothing insane about feeling good."

He let his teeth scrape over the top of Dal's spine, a spot he'd discovered was incredibly sensitive. "I just know what you need."

Dal cried out, went up on tiptoe, ass pushing out. "I still can't believe you saw me. I'm so careful..."

"Not careful enough." Thank God. He couldn't imagine missing out on this.

His hands slid down Dal's thighs and then over to rub the soap over the man's balls. Then he pushed it back behind them, sliding the soap along the tiny patch of smooth, sensitive skin. The rings there shifted and slid, clicked together like tiny castanets.

"My favorite surprise," he murmured, sliding the hand without the soap down there to twist and tug.

He brought the soap up to Dal's curls, foaming them up. "Gonna let me shave you? Let me see?"

"Right before I leave? No. No, consider it something to look forward to. After Tokyo."

He growled a little, biting at the back of Dal's neck. "Tease."

His fingers slid through the dark curls, pressing against Dal's skin as if trying to see the tattoo like it was Braille.

"I put out." Dal chuckled, wiggling and

moaning low.

He nodded -- couldn't deny that. "You do. I'm just an impatient man." One who wasn't used to being denied either.

He took a step back, hands sliding to soap up Dal's back, rubbing the soap nice and hard along the lean length, the pretty muscles. He was saving that ass for second to last, and Dal's cock for the end. Dal's muscles rippled, that incredible responsiveness enough to make him ache. He bent to slide the soap along Dal's legs, fingers sliding along the insides of Dal's thighs on his way up. The soap slid along Dale's crack and he pushed close, his prick gliding along the slick skin. His hands circled the perfect ass, holding and squeezing and soaping.

"Could touch you forever," he admitted. "Soft, hard, leave marks..."

"Make it hard for me to sit in those interminable meetings, then."

"Oh, I plan to leave you with a memory or two of me," he murmured, hands sliding around to start soaping up Dal's prick.

"Did you see the glove I had, baby? All covered in little rubber points." His voice grew husky, deep. "Your shirt and suit jacket are going to make you insane."

"Too bad you won't be there to see..."

"But I'll know." Fuck, just thinking about it now had him all worked up. "And our paths will cross now and then, Dal." He'd make sure of it. Meetings with the prim and proper Scott Daly would never, ever be the same again.

Secrets, Skin and Leather

"You think so?"

Fuck, yes. He knew it. They might kill him, but he knew it.

He palmed Dal's cock, the soap making it slick and easy as he stroked. He kept rubbing his cock along Dal's ass in the same rhythm, groaning. "I know so. Damn. Dal. Wanna bend you over the board table and fuck you raw."

"Mmm. Never done that..." Dal just danced for him, sliding and rocking, undulating for him.

He pictured the staid Scott in his mind and chuckled. "No, I'll just bet you haven't."

Groaning, he moved faster, his prick rubbing and sliding. He dropped the soap, looking for where he'd left that studded rubber glove. He was driven to give Dal as much sensation as he could.

"What are you looking... oh, mmm... feels good..."

"Yeah. Yeah, it does." He caught sight of the glove on the edge of the tub and he bit the base of Dal's neck before making a grab for it, only losing a moment or two of rubbing and tugging.

"Looking for this," he murmured, slipping the glove on and letting it skitter along Dal's belly.

"That's..." Dal shivered, grabbed his hand to look. "That's something."

"It's going to leave the most interesting pattern all over your body." He stroked Dal's palm lightly.

He pressed a little harder, just barely pricking the skin. "But I won't intentionally draw blood. This time."

"No blood." Dal watched, eyes heated, fascinated. He nodded. It was about sensation, not pain. Or at least not necessarily about pain.

Watching, still rubbing his prick almost idly against Dal's ass, he stroked the glove along Dal's right hip and down over his thigh, watching as the pointed studs left behind tiny scratches that quickly became welts. Dal groaned, pulled away, the water running down to soothe the skin. He licked at the sweet spot on Dal's neck, giving Dal another sensation to focus on, one that was easier. Then he moved the glove over Dal's belly again, almost bouncing it along the tight muscles.

"Where... where did you find that thing?"

"I don't think I should give away all my secrets, Dal, do you?" Chuckling, the sound husky, a testament to how affected he was, he swept the glove up and bounced it off one nipple and then dragged it over the other.

"Fuck." Dal groaned, pulled away with a shudder. "Fuck, that stings."

He slid his ungloved hand down to wrap around Dal's prick. Oh, yeah, still nice and hard. He stroked it, thumb rubbing over the tip, as he bounced the prickles over Dal's nipple again. Dal jerked and shivered, arching into his hand from the waist down and pulling away from the waist up. He touched a few more times, pricking those hips and thighs again, the belly, Dal's ribs.

Then he tossed off the glove and let his hands wander, feeling the different welts and scratches he'd left, touching lightly and then more firmly, pressing against this welt, rubbing over that one. Dal's tension melted, the man melting against him, undulating against his body.

"Hedonist," he accused. He would have to play with the pain/pleasure dynamic when they had more time, push Dal's limits as well as his own.

He pinched the more abused nipple, making sure his fingernails scraped over a welt. Dal's ass pushed back against his cock, rubbing good and hard, trying to drive him mad. It was going to work, too, because the fucking condoms were all in the bedroom. Groaning, he twisted Dal's other nipple and rubbed the firm six-pack.

"We gotta move this back to the bed."

"Do we? You wanting something?" Little tease. Little fuck.

"Your ass and you know it, baby." He growled a little, biting at Dal's earlobe. "All the fucking stuff is in the bedroom." He'd make sure that little mistake wasn't repeated in the future.

"Uh-huh. You should've thought." That ass moved faster, muscles tight.

He couldn't not respond, couldn't not rub back, his prick sliding along Dal's cock as he pressed in close. Groaning, he pushed his hand between them and pushed his cock down, into the space between Dal's thighs. "Squeeze. Fuck, baby, squeeze."

"Hell, yes." Dal's legs clamped down around his prick, wet and slick and just what he needed.

"Uh-huh." He rested his forehead on Dal's back, his hand working Dal's prick, rough and quick, as his hips moved, thrusting into the tunnel between Dal's legs. His eyes closed, sparks dancing behind his lids. Their skin slapped together, the water splashing between them, bouncing up between them.

"Fuck, Dal. Baby." He whimpered, free hand moving to feel the welts and scrapes on Dal's body. "Gonna make me come, baby."

"Good. Good, come on. Show me."

Yeah, he could do that. He pushed harder, the sound of their skin meeting sweet. Crying out, he came, the orgasm coming up from his toes and shooting out of him. Dal moaned, letting him ride it out, still rubbing, still holding him between those strong legs. It lasted and lasted and then it was over and he melted against Dal, letting the man support him.

"Fuck," he muttered, hand still working Dal's prick without him even thinking about it.

"Yeah." Dal moaned, leaned against the marble, hips just barely working.

He swept his thumb over the tip of Dal's prick, pushing in a bit, letting his nail dig. "Your turn."

He tightened his grip and his free hand started to wander again, finding the welts and scratches he'd left on Dal's belly, caressing them. He could live on Dal's whimpers, the way the man's head tossed, the working of the long throat. He licked at a bite mark on Dal's shoulder, tongue tracing where his teeth had bruised the skin.

So damned fine. His hand tightened -- he didn't want to let go -- and his free hand slid

Secrets, Skin and Leather

down to cup and tug on Dal's balls, little finger reaching back to snag on the rings buried in Dal's flesh. Oh, yes. That earned him a groan, Dal going up on his toes and stretching.

"That's it, baby. Give it to me." He tugged harder, twisted the little ring and squeezed Dal's balls just enough for the man to really feel it. Heat sprayed out over his hand, Dal just melting back against him with a groan. "Oh, yeah, just like that." He kept stroking gently, pulling out another sweet shudder.

Finally, he let go of Dal's balls and his cock and just held the man, the water spraying over them, warm and good as they stood together.

"I'm glad you saw me."

He smiled, the words warming him inside. "Yeah, me, too."

He nuzzled against Dal's neck. "Me, too."

Chapter Three

Fuck, he was tired.
Worn out.
Jet lagged.
Ready to go home for a two-week vacation -- he fully intended to sleep for the first week and then party his ass off for the second.

First, though, Scott had to get through this interminable cocktail party.

Go him.

Honestly, something called a "cocktail" party should be more fun.

Not that he'd gotten much cock lately. He'd gone to London, then Tokyo, and returned home to a cryptic message about Dillon being away on business indefinitely. Well, he'd been dumped enough to know what that meant. Still, he'd turned it to his advantage. He'd just gone to Athens and then Sydney and now, thank God, he was home.

The usual suspects were all in attendance -- CEOs and their sycophants, lawyers, brokers like himself. Except there wasn't anyone here like him, now, was there. Not really. The noise of male voices was intercut with the occasional shriller tones of the women and the infernal noise from the string quartet in the corner. Waiters dressed in tuxes circulated with trays of little snacks that weren't really very filling, only teased his appetite and then didn't fill his belly.

But Bob Hargrove was a good client and Scott couldn't leave until the old man had made his little speech. Which, if Hargrove ran true to form, wouldn't be for another hour or so.

"Well, well, well. It looks like they'll let anyone in these days." The voice was low, husky. Intimately familiar despite the fact that he hadn't heard it in a couple of months.

A tall glass with a lime wedge appeared in front of him, a strong, manicured hand holding it.

"Club soda, right?" There was a teasing note in that voice, but it was buried under a huskiness he'd heard a lot in three short days eight weeks ago.

"I... Yes. Yes, thank you. It's kind of you to remember." Fuck, the man was beautiful. Dillon's eyes were as dark as he remembered, the look in them hot, wanton and totally at odds with the conservative dark grey suit.

He was looked up and down, and he swore Dillon could see right through his suit, right into him. "You never used that number."

"I had a message that you were otherwise disposed. I wasn't sure if our business had been completed or not." He sipped his drink, not even cracking a smile.

One of Dillon's eyebrows went up. "You've never had to reschedule a meeting before?"

"I have. I admit, I've only just arrived back in the country this morning, so I hadn't had a chance to reschedule." He resisted the urge to bounce, to touch, to stroke his belly and remind Dillon of the corsets, the play.

Dillon took a step closer. They weren't touching, but he swore he could feel the heat of Dillon's body, smell the man's musk. "What a coincidence; today's the first day I haven't had to put out fires."

"How interesting. I begin a two-week vacation once this party comes to an end."

Dillon's nostrils flared. "Indeed? I believe my own schedule could possibly be cleared for a day, or seven."

Before he could reply, a balding man he'd seen but couldn't name came up, clapping Dillon on the shoulder. "Walsh! You've missed our last two golf games. Not avoiding me are you?"

Dillon laughed, the sound fake -- Scott knew that now, knew it from hearing the real laughter. "Bill. Not at all. In fact, I could have used your sage advice the other day when the Swanson deal blew up." Dillon turned to Scott. "But I'm being rude. Bill, this is Scott Daly. Scott – Bill Sorenson." It was amazing, the difference in Dillon's voice now that they weren't alone. The husky, intimate tone had been replaced by a cool blandness.

"I'm pleased to meet you, sir." He made pointless small talk, listening for things that would make money, but ignoring the rest.

Well, maybe he wasn't ignoring Dillon...

Several more people joined them and Dillon's voice droned in with the others, but he could feel those dark eyes on him, could feel Dillon undressing him with those eyes, could almost feel the man touching him.

Scott excused himself, found a bathroom where he could wash his face, make sure his contacts were in, make sure his prick wasn't obvious.

The door opened just as he thought he had himself under control, Dillon standing in the doorway. The man hummed, the door closing behind him. The snick of the lock was loud.

"Walsh." He blinked, hands still sliding over the towel to dry them.

Dillon shook his head. "Not at the moment." The man stalked toward him, eyes nearly setting the place on fire.

"I don't play in public." His cock jerked, filled.

Dillon made a show of looking around. "We're not *in* public. And I won't leave a mark where anyone can see it."

"Bastard." He licked his lips, breath coming faster, heart starting to beat.

Dillon just nodded at the insult and stepped right up to him, hands sliding beneath his jacket, grabbing his waist, fingers searching to see if he was naked beneath his shirt. He sucked in his belly, muscles rippling as Dillon's hands found skin. Oh, fuck. Hot.

Dillon's face came close to his, lips stopping just short of his. Their breath mingled, hot and flavored with the whiskey Dillon'd been drinking. The dark eyes were huge so close to his, Dillon's every breath loud. The long fingers slid up, found one of his nipples and pinched hard. "Come to the beach house."

"When?" His toes curled, fingers curling into fists.

"I can have a limousine pick us up in an hour." Dillon's fingers dragged back down to his waist, slid across his belly. Scott could smell the want rising from Dillon's skin.

"You'll have to feed me. I'm starving." Exhausted. Horny as fuck.

"Me, too." Dillon's tongue slid across his lips. "What's your pleasure?"

"Something private, easy." He moaned, his eyes rolling, lips following that heated tongue. "I can't do this."

Dillon stepped back at his words, checked his cufflinks, all business. But when those eyes cut back to him, the heat in them was still there, not banked even a little bit. "There will be a limousine at the corner of Fourth and Swanson in exactly an hour. Be there. You'll have everything you need in it."

"I'll let Dal know." He thumped his cock, turned back to the sink to splash water on his cheeks.

Dillon's chuckle was husky and went right to his prick, making it try to perk right back up again. "Don't miss that limo." With that, Dillon shot the bolt back to unlock the door and let himself out.

No. No, he wouldn't miss it. Not a chance. He met his eyes in the mirror, the dark dull and still, hiding him away. Dal wouldn't miss it at all.

He couldn't see Dillon anywhere when he went back out, his cock only marginally under control. Bob Hargrove's speech took care of that little matter, the man wrapping it up just about the time Scott had to head out to walk the three blocks to the corner where he was supposed to get picked up by Dillon's limo.

He wrapped his coat around him, the wind blowing and chilly, sharp enough to be almost cold. Still, no one he knew followed him. No one saw him. No one even looked.

A dark grey stretch limo with tinted windows pulled up to the intersection as the got there, a tall, grey haired man in a chauffeur's uniform coming around. "Mr. Daly?"

"Yes. Good evening." He nodded, let the man open the door and then slipped in.

It was dark inside, the privacy window already in place. A low purr sounded as soon as the door closed, a hand wrapping around his wrist and tugging him against a hard body.

"Hey." He moaned, twisting to bring their mouths together, to bring their bodies together.

"Hey," breathed Dillon into his mouth.

Then they were kissing, Dillon's tongue parting his lips, pushing in like the man was starving and he was number one on the menu. He wrapped his lips around Dillon's tongue, pulling and humming, sucking good and hard. Dillon groaned, fingers tugging his tie loose and ripping open his shirt. As soon as his skin was exposed, Dillon's fingers were on it.

His nerves felt like they were alight, just

burning and sparking, suddenly alive. He could feel the heat of Dillon's prick against his thigh, the expensive fabric of their suits in the way of what he wanted, what he needed. His jacket was pushed off, his shirt torn right off his back. Dillon's hands landed on his ass and tugged him close. He shifted until he was straddling those strong thighs, bending down to kiss the man hard enough his lip split.

Dillon growled, lapping at his lips and then diving back into the kiss. The talented fingers worked on his belt, drawing it through the loops on his pants. The button on his pants went flying as Dillon tugged it open.

"You're Hell on the wardrobe." He groaned, fingers tangling in Dillon's thin shirt.

"You aren't going to need clothes where we're going. His zipper was pulled down, Dillon's hand reaching into his pants and wrapping around his prick. "Gonna shave you, too. Finally see what you're hiding."

"You are?" Fuck, he needed. Right now. "Are you sure?"

"Oh, yeah. I'm fucking sure." Dillon started jacking him off, hand quick and rough around his flesh.

"Yeah..." His head fell back, throat working as his balls drew up tight. Maybe he'd have to hold back on that, keep Dillon guessing, wanting.

Dillon took it as an invitation, mouth latching onto his neck, right below his Adam's apple. Teeth first, and then lips and tongue, sharp

Secrets, Skin and Leather

followed by smooth and wet and hot. He bucked and groaned, shooting into Dillon's hand, heat just flooding him. Dillon's groan made his skin vibrate, that mouth still latched onto him; the mark was going to be dark. The hand around his cock kept moving, sliding slickly now, pulling out shudders and shivers and another small spurt.

God, he was melted.

Completely.

One hand stroked down Dillon's spine, trying to touch, but he was all shivers and moans.

Dillon groaned for him, hand grabbing his and tugging it to Dillon's crotch. "My turn," whispered Dillon. "God, I've wanted you for fucking *weeks*." He could feel Dillon's prick, hard and insistent, tenting the dress slacks.

"Thought you'd changed your mind." He fumbled, finally getting the zipper down without ruining Dillon altogether.

Another groan answered him, Dillon pushing up into his hand, prick like velvet-covered steel. "You'll find once I set my course, I stay it," muttered Dillon. "Was just fucking busy."

"Yeah. It'll be relatively slow 'til after Christmas, now." He shoved Dillon's shirt away, teeth sinking in to scrape against that fine-grained skin.

Dillon jerked, body pushing up into his mouth, hands finding his hips and wrapping around them, sliding up along his sides. "Got something for you."

"Hmm? What?" That prick was enough for him, for now.

"Corset. To hold you tight. Beach house... has lots toys." Dillon was gasping the words out, hips working, pushing the fine prick through his fingers. "Oh, fuck. Dal. Yeah."

"Uh-huh." He nodded, agreeing wholeheartedly. Yes. Toys. Anything. "Come on, now. Give it up."

"You wa--" Dillon's words turned into a shout, heat spraying over his fingers, the scent good and strong, filling the limousine.

Dillon slumped back, hands wrapped around his waist, pulling him up against the solid chest that rose and fell with each quick breath. He hummed, leaned right in. Warm. Good. Yeah. Now that the urgency had faded some, now that they were both quiet and still as they caught their breath, he could feel the slight motions of the car, could just barely hear it. They were going fast, rushing through the darkness -- they'd obviously already left the city.

"This was a most pleasant surprise," murmured Dillon, hands traveling over him, mapping him maybe, feeling him up definitely. "Almost as good as that first time I saw you and realized who you were."

"Only almost?" He was floating.

Dillon hummed, hands continuing to touch and slide over him. "Well... it's close. Last time there was several weeks of planning and anticipation to build my appetite. This time..." Dillon shifted, hips pushing, lifting him momentarily. "Well, there was far less time to anticipate once I saw you, but then I knew exactly how good it was going to be when we came together." Dillon leaned back in, mouth sliding along his neck, tongue flicking the mark that had been left just a few minutes earlier.

He whimpered, nerves firing. "Mmm. Again."

"Gonna paint you in marks, Dal. From head to toe." Dillon growled, and bit down on his skin, teeth scraping over the mark.

"Fuck!" He moaned, twisting, pulling away before pushing right back.

Dillon laughed, the sound low, sexy as fuck. "Oh, yeah, baby, you love that, don't you." Dillon's teeth worried a spot just below the first.

"Uh-huh. Damn..." His toes curled, lips parting as Dillon bit again.

"Bought you supper," murmured Dillon. "You can have it. After." Strong fingers dug into his hips, hard enough to leave bruises.

"After what?" Oh. Food. He could eat.

"After I mark you, baby. Leave reminders of me all over your body." Dillon's fingers slid over to his ass, the touch firm, hard, making him ache just a little.

"I can't believe you talked me into this without even going home." Well, okay. He could believe it.

He wanted.

Dillon snorted. "What's waiting for you at home, Dal, when everything you want is right here?"

"Contact lens holder and toothbrush."

Dillon's laughter was husky, sexy. "Those are replaceable, baby." A sharp bite bruised his skin just over his heart. He groaned, hips bucking, rocking against Dillon's thigh. "God, you're sexy." Dillon's lips wrapped around his nipple, teeth worrying it, tongue playing the very tip over and over again.

Fuck, that was hot. Burning. Sharp. More. Please, more.

Dillon bit down hard, thumbs rubbing the join where his thighs met his body, fingers tugging at his pubes. He arched, easing the sting and the pull, following the touch. Dillon growled, mouth sliding across his chest, leaving random stinging bites before winding up at his other nipple. The touches started out soft, licks and nibbles, teases. Then Dillon bit, catching the skin around his nipple.

"Fuck!" His cock jerked, threatening to go hard again.

"We will. I promise. Again and again." Each of Dillon's words was punctuated with a lick, or a bite, the order random, keeping each bite sharp and new.

"Uh-huh. After we. Uh. Eat." Damn, his nerves were buzzing.

"Oh, yeah, gonna eat you right up, Dal. Every single inch." Dillon's voice was little more than a husky growl, the sound just going straight to his cock.

"You're going to get me revved up again." Again. Hell, he was aching.

"I certainly hope so." Dillon's hands slid up around his back, grabbing his shoulders as another bite landed on his skin, just above his belly. Dillon's lips closed around his skin, began to suck; this mark was sure to be dark and lurid.

"I'll look like a leper." Like a well-fucked leper who was fucking happy as Hell.

Dillon laughed. "You'll look like you're mine." Dillon's eyes glittered up at him in the almost darkness.

He looked right back, not backing down a bit. "You'd better make sure you can handle me."

"Haven't I already proved that?" Dillon was back to growling, fingers moving to tweak one nipple, the other hand sliding into his still undone pants and tugging on his rings.

"Uhn... I may have forgotten. You'll have to remind me." Fuck, he did love a good tease, a good, firm touch.

"Oh, I will, will I?" Dillon's fingers slid beyond his rings, jostling his gland from the outside.

"Yes..." Dal wasn't sure what he was agreeing to.

Dillon purred and slid his fingers further back, nails dragging lightly against his hole, the tip of one finger pushing in. Dal tilted his hips, trying to get more, feel more, get more of that touch.

"Hungry, baby." That finger pushed in to the second knuckle and wiggled.

"Uh...uh-*huh*." He jerked and groaned as electricity shot through him. Goddamn.

"Fuck. Sexy. Here, suck on this." Dillon pushed two fingers against his lips, wriggling them just like the finger inside him did. "Make 'em good and wet, baby." Dal latched on, sucking hard as his eyes closed, focusing on making it feel good. Dillon groaned, thumb pushing against his gland from the outside, the finger inside him just barely brushing it. "Yeah. Just like that. Fuck."

He just nodded, head bobbing, fellating those fingers, pretending they were Dillon's prick.

Dillon's hips started moving, thrusting up, so it was like he was riding that prick, too. "Want you. So fucking bad." God, yes. He knew. He wanted Dillon inside him, hard and deep enough that he could *taste* it.

Dillon's fingers slid out of his mouth with a pop, the finger in his ass disappearing as well. He wasn't empty for long, though, the two fingers he'd wetted pushing into him without any fanfare, Dillon just taking his ass.

"Fuck, yes. Please." He wasn't too proud to ask for what he needed.

"I love the way you beg." Dillon fucked him hard with those fingers, mouth finding one of his nipples again and setting off to drive him crazy.

"Ask. Not beg. More." His balls drew up tight.

Dillon laughed and if the sound wasn't so husky and desperate he might have thought Dillon was laughing *at* him. "You say to-ma-to, I say to-mah-to." Suddenly there were three fingers in him, jabbing sharply, hitting his gland as they pushed deep.

Dal's head slammed back and his hips bucked up as he shot, entire body awash in pure fucking heat.

Dillon groaned. "Damn. You were supposed to wait for me. I'm gonna have to get a cock ring on you pronto." Still, Dillon's fingers kept working him, stretching and sliding inside him, pulling out one shudder after another, not letting it end. His eyes rolled, body working those fingers. He let himself imagine taking Dillon's hand, taking that bare cock deep. Fantasies.

"Sweet. Fuck. Need." Dillon's fingers disappeared.

Their breathing was loud in the confines of the limo, but he could still hear the crinkle of the condom wrapper as it was opened, and a moment later, Dillon was shifting him, the blunt, beautiful heat of the man's cock pressing against his hole.

"Yeah..." He pushed down and took Dillon in, tip to root, just moaning low at the burn.

"Fuck. Shit. Yes." Dillon nodded, voice choked, strained. "So fucking tight. Hot." Dillon's hands wrapped around his waist, holding him tight as if he were wearing a flesh corset. "Ride, Dal. Make me come."

Dal nodded, lip caught between his teeth as he started moving, riding Dillon good and hard. Yeah. Yeah, like that. Damn. Dillon regressed to groans and grunts, mouth sliding on his skin, teeth catching now and then, sending sharp sensations shooting through him. He squeezed Dillon hard, moaning as sensation poured through him.

Dillon jerked and cried out, starting to hump

up, meeting him each time he came down, slamming their bodies together. "Dal. Dal." His name was chanted over and over, the sound growing more and more ragged.

"Uh-huh. Right here." Good. So fucking *good*.

"Gonna. Soon. Dal." Dillon's fingers wrapped tighter around his waist, pulling him down hard. Faster and faster, and then Dillon was shouting, cock throbbing inside him, filling the condom.

Dillon slumped, gasping. He groaned and leaned in, eyes just dropping closed, exhausted, balls to bones.

Dillon's arms wrapped around his back, held him tight. "Oh, baby. The things I am going to do to you in the next two weeks." Dillon chuckled.

"Promises, promis..." He sank into sleep before the sentence finished, comfortable and happy right where he was.

***

Dal dozed in Dillon's arms until the chauffeur's voice came over the intercom. "Five minutes, sir."

Then Dillon hummed and stretched a little, fingers dancing along his spine. "Time to wake up, baby. Time to see where you're going to have your mind blown."

Dal purred and snuggled. "So warm, love."

Dillon hummed. "Yeah, baby. We're here though. Your shirt's toast, but you can wear my

Secrets, Skin and Leather

leather jacket."

"Mmm... where's here?" He stretched, body rippling.

Dillon licked his lips, obviously enjoying the movement, letting his hands linger and caress. "The beach house in Maine. On the beach. We should be pulling up in about three minutes. And then you can finally have that supper."

"Oh, that sounds heavenly. Sorry about crashing."

"Oh, I took it as a compliment, baby. I wore you out." Dillon gave Dal a wink, hand sliding down to goose his ass.

"Mmmhmm." Dal shifted away from the pinch, leaned to nip Dillon's lip. "What's for supper?"

"Well, I had these lovely high-end sandwiches, but I'm guessing they're a little stale at this point. Barbara, my housekeeper here at the beach house, promised me a lobster feast when we arrived." Dillon slid his hands around to the front of Dal's pants, sliding the filling cock in and carefully doing up the zipper.

"Mmm. Lobster. I'm a fan." Dal leaned in and nuzzled Dillon's throat.

The car rolled to a stop and the chauffeur's voice came over the intercom again. "We've arrived, sir."

Grinning at Dal, humming a little at the nuzzling, Dillon reached over and pressed the button. "Thank you, Brenan. We'll see ourselves out." He let the button go and raised an eyebrow at Dal. "Unless you'd like to put on a show?"

"No, I'm good." Dal grinned at him, sliding back. "I have a reputation, you know."

Dillon laughed, hand sliding along his ass. "I know. Oh, baby, I know." Dillon put his leather jacket around Dal's shoulders. "You should always smell of leather."

"Not sex?" Of course, leather and sex were close to the same.

Dillon purred, the sound rich and sexy. "I do like the way you think, Dal. Leather *and* sex." Dillon's words echoed his thoughts.

"Mmmhmm. Now feed me and let me take these contacts out."

"Oh, yes. I want your real eyes, Dal. I want the real you, not the staid facsimile you present to the world."

Dillon led him into a large cottage with a wrap-around porch. Of course, "cottage" didn't really do the place justice. The floors were polished hardwood, and a woman met them at the door. "Mr. Walsh, sir. Welcome back."

"Thank you, Barbara. I asked for supper to be ready for us."

"Yes, sir. In the dining room. I believe you'll find the menu matches your requests."

"Excellent. Why don't you go home to your family? We can mange to serve ourselves."

Her "very good, sir, thank you," followed them down the hall to the dining room where a feast was laid out on the table.

"Good Lord. There's enough for an army." Dal grabbed a spear of cantaloupe, looking at the rustic, masculine, yet incredibly rich decor in

Secrets, Skin and Leather

wines and blues and deep, deep greens. Lovely.

"You said you were hungry." Dillon pulled a chair out from the table and sat, patting his thighs. "On my lap, baby. I'll feed you."

He hummed, straddling Dillon's legs, his dress slacks pulling. "Okay. Feed me."

Dillon's hands slid along his thighs. "Take out those terrible contacts first. No more hiding behind any of your masks. You're *mine* for the next two weeks."

His cheek heated and his thighs went tight. Fuck, that was sexy, being seen. "You don't like them dark?"

"I like them dark. With need. With want. Not with colored contacts. Take them out, Dal. Now." Dillon growled a little. "Now."

"Pushy bitch." He popped the contacts out, the little disks dropping into his hands.

Dillon's hand wrapped around his, closing it around the contacts, crushing them. "I just know what I want. I know what you want, too."

"I want you." He met Dillon's eyes, letting his pleasure show. "And food."

Dillon chuckled and unfolded his hand, taking the contacts out and tossing them nonchalantly over his shoulder. "I know."

Eyes on his, Dillon moved close, reaching behind him for something on the table. His lips were licked, and then Dillon sat back again and a chunk of lobster dipped in garlic butter was held out.

"Mmm... yummy." He leaned forward, teeth stealing the morsel. Oh. Decadent. Sweet.

Dillon purred, tongue licking at his lips, then it slipped between them, stealing the flavor right out of his mouth. "More?" Dillon asked, voice husky.

"Mmmhmm. Yes. Please." He was a huge fan of more.

This time Dillon put the lobster in his own mouth and moved in, pressed their lips together. Mmm. Tasty. Dal relaxed into the kiss, the explosion of sweetness almost like a pastry, with the butter and garlic to save it, make it savory. They shared the bite, Dillon's hums and his tongue sliding and slipping in Dal's mouth.

"Something a little sharper this time?" Dillon asked as he broke the kiss, reaching for more food.

It was more lobster, but this time an explosion of tart lemon covered the sweetness of the meat. It made him gasp and lick his lips to get more of the citrus, more of the bright flavor.

"So do you like it better with the lemon or are you just jonesing on the surprise?" Dillon asked him.

"I don't know. Give me another bite to test."

Dillon laughed softly, and another chunk of lemon-dipped lobster was popped into Dal's mouth, Dillon smiling at him, eyes dark and hot. Mmm. Tart and rich and refreshing, not as decadent as the butter, but cleansing to the palette.

"I like them both."

"Oh, yes. You like it all." Dillon licked his lips again and then a large shrimp dipped in what looked like tartar sauce appeared between their mouths. Dillon started nibbling on one side.

Dal laughed, tickled. This was one of the most interesting meals he'd had in months. He ate from the other side, their mouths meeting in the middle. It was sweet and spicy at the same time, and the three grapes that Dillon popped into his mouth after were fresh and cooling.

"More? Or are you ready for dessert?"

"Mmm... something crunchy." He was enjoying this too much to stop.

"Oh, crunchy." Dillon snapped his teeth together, chuckled. "I think we can find something crunchy..."

A moment later a fried wonton was pressed to his lips, salty and sharp with the flavor of soya sauce. Oh, yum. He bit deep, moaning, rocking a little with it. Okay, crunchy was good.

"Fuck, you're so goddamned sensual." Dillon's fingers slid along his lower lip. "Makes me want to eat you right up."

Another wonton was offered, this one dipped in something sweet with a bit of a bite underneath it. "Oh." That made him lick his lips, made him thirsty. "Wine?"

"I think we've got something a step up from that." Dillon leaned against him, arm stretching behind him to grab what turned out to be a bottle of champagne.

"I just need to make it pop." Dillon winked and worked carefully at the cork.

"You're pretty good at making it..." The cork popped, champagne bubbling out, making them both laugh.

Dillon only poured out one glass, tipping a finger into the liquid and painting his lips with it. Then Dillon took a mouthful and brought their mouths together. Oh, sweet. Dal reached up, cupped Dillon's jaw and purred as the liquid poured into his lips, bubbling and burning and tingling. Dillon fed the sound back to him along with the champagne, one hand sliding down his back and bringing his groin in tight against Dillon's.

The kiss continued long after the champagne was gone, Dillon's eyes so dark as they stared into his own. They were pressed together, hips to shoulder, both of them moving, rubbing nice and easy. They shared breath and taste, tongues working together, slipping and sliding and dancing. They stopped only long enough for Dillon to take another mouthful of the bubbly to share with him. He laughed as the bubbles tickled his nose, and he relaxed into Dillon, just enjoying the ability to touch.

Dillon purred. "Feels good, doesn't it, baby? Knowing we have all the time in the world." That low, throaty chuckle was so sexy. "Well, two weeks. Almost the same thing in our world."

"Yeah. Stolen time." Things were so intense, so sudden, so sharp between them.

"As long as we're not arrested." Dillon grinned, reaching behind him again and offering another large chunk of lobster with garlic butter.

"Scott Daly *doesn't* get arrested." Dal, on the other hand? Well, no. No arresting. It wasn't his

Secrets, Skin and Leather

style.

Dillon looked around, seemed to be searching for something. "I don't see any Scott Daly here, baby. Just us perverts."

"Nobody here but us chickens?" He leaned back, grabbed a stalk of asparagus, and started nibbling.

"That's right." Dillon leaned forward and bit the end of Dal's asparagus. The man's hands were on him again, pushing the leather jacket off his shoulders.

"Asparagus thief." Mmm... the place was warm enough to be comfortable, cool enough to make his nipples peak.

"Told you I was a perv." The tip of Dillon's tongue touched one of his nipples, then cold air blew over it.

"Oh." His belly went tight, pecs jerking and bunching up. Yum.

"Oh, yeah." Dillon grabbed a lemon and squeezed it over Dal's skin, the juices running over his nipple. Then Dillon's tongue followed the same path, flat, dragging over his skin. "Mmm... better even than lobster."

"Perv." Lemon-flavored businessman. Hrm. Possibly better than buttered businessman... Or maybe not.

"Real perversion would be stuffing grapes up your ass."

"That would be a little... squishy." Man, that was a weird visual.

Dillon chuckled and sprayed more lemon on Dal's skin, licking along his breastbone and over to his other nipple. "We don't want squishy." Dillon's tongue circled his nipple, and then his teeth struck, biting. "We want hard."

Dal was fairly sure he should say something, he just couldn't find the words. He groaned, arching up into Dillon's mouth.

"Someone's still hungry," murmured Dillon. Teeth and tongue worked his nipple, sucking and biting and pulling up heat.

"The... the lobster is good." Hungry. Fuck. Hot. He leaned back, heart pounding, hips and ass sliding on Dillon's slacks.

"Lobster..." Dillon laughed, and backed off, dammit. "If that's really what you want, I can accommodate you." The dark eyes twinkled at him as Dillon reached for another bite of lobster, rubbed it over his lips, coating them with garlic butter. He bit at the lobster and if he caught Dillon's fingers, so much the better. "You want more than just lobster." Dillon's fingers lingered, played with his lips, dipped into his mouth to run over his teeth.

"I do." He wanted everything, from fucking on this long, expensive table to exploring this beautiful beach house.

"Good." The word was little more than a growl, and Dillon's mouth attached onto his collarbone, sucking hard. Shit. His eyes rolled as heat rippled through him, wave after wave just getting bigger.

Dillon's fingers mapped his body, dragging over his skin as they explored, moving steadily downward. All the while Dillon's mouth worked.

Secrets, Skin and Leather

"You are enough to drive a man mad." His slacks were bunched up around his cock, trapping him.

"Uh-huh." Dillon's mouth was too busy for more than that, moving from his collarbone to his breastbone. That wicked tongue flicked back and forth across his skin as Dillon's fingers slid around his waistband.

"I... I can't touch you like this, Dillon." He couldn't do anything but hold on.

"Can't have that." One of Dillon's arms wrapped around him, hand grabbing his ass, the other swept the table behind him. Then he was lifted, Dillon pushing him up so he was sitting on the table, Dillon standing between his legs. "Better, baby?"

"Fuck, yes." He reached out, fingers working Dillon's shirt open.

"Fuck, love the way you touch me." Dillon's mouth was on his again, tongue pushing into his mouth, the kiss growing hard, fast.

It was so easy to just lose himself in the kiss, fingers tangled in Dillon's shirt and tugging hard. The buttons popped, went flying with sweet little pings against the floor, the dining room table. Dillon's growl filled his mouth, while the long fingers pulled open his pants, undid the zipper. Mmm. That was fun. He pulled again, biting at Dillon's lips.

The expensive shirt tore under his pulls, Dillon groaning, jerking against him. Dillon's long fingers pushed aside his pants, touched the tip of his cock, slid down the length with a light, easy touch that was belied by the ragged moans that sounded as if they came deep from Dillon's belly. He arched up into the touch, ass pressing back into the table.

"Want you. No." Dillon shook his head, dark eyes staring into his. "Need to have you." His pants were tugged off his ass, pulled down off his legs, and then Dillon's hands grabbed his ass and tugged him to the edge of the table.

"Come on then. Remind me of what you have." He could push back. He loved pushing back.

Dillon growled, the sound low and needy and so fucking hot. It sent a shiver down Dal's back, made his cock jerk against his belly.

"I have you," Dillon told him, mouth covering his. He was bent back over the table, Dillon's hand pushing his legs apart, fingers finding his rings. They hadn't been played with in weeks, the skin sensitive and begging more touches, more sensation. Dillon's fingers slid and twisted, turned them, tugged them, gave him what he needed. The man's tongue echoed his fingers, fucking Dal's mouth.

"Undress me. Get me ready." The words were growled, a tube and a condom package pressed into his hand.

"Bossy." He sat up, started working buttons and zippers, ass slipping on the slick table.

"I just know what I want." Dillon's teeth nipped at his earlobe, at his neck. Hot lips and wet tongue slid on his skin, the touches not quite distracting him from what he was doing.

Secrets, Skin and Leather

A sweet hiss sounded once he'd freed Dillon's cock, the thick heat pushing into his hand. He ripped the condom open, dipping his chin and watching as he worked the condom down over the heavy, full prick. So pretty.

"Oh, fuck, yeah. Hurry, baby." One of Dillon's fingers slid in behind his rings, circled his hole and then pushed right in. "Tight. Hot. Want in."

"Uh-huh." He could get behind that. In front of it. Whatever. Dal spread, heels swinging, trying to get purchase on something.

Dillon grabbed the lube and then a second finger pushed into him, working him open, stretching him for that cock. Dillon's free hand pushed against one of his thighs, helping him get his heel up on the table.

"Oh, yeah." He nodded, that's what he needed. Just that.

"Look at you, all spread out for me." Dillon's eyes were dark, dragging over his body like a physical touch before meeting his again. "Can't wait any longer. Won't."

Dillon's fingers disappeared, the thick prick there a moment later, pushing at his hole. God, Dillon was big. And hard. And so damned hot. Dal made this sound, deep and rough and raw, just an absolute agreement and encouragement. Dillon's mouth met his, tongue pushing in, insistent and sure, just like the cock that pressed into him, spreading him wide. Grunts and groans, soft moans, each one filled him as Dillon began to fuck him, the table rocking with them, creaking.

Fuck, yes. He wrapped his free leg around Dillon's hip, moaning and pulling. Just like that.

"Oh, fuck. Been too long." Dillon grunted, one hand wrapping around his hip, tugging him into each thrust.

Their movements sped, grew more urgent. "Gonna do so many things to you," groaned Dillon. "Fuck you raw."

"Promise?" He could handle that. He had two weeks to recover.

"You know it, baby." Dillon's voice stroked over him, the man's eyes dark, boring into his own.

Their flesh slapped together, the sound loud, joined by their harsh gasps as they worked together, Dillon's thrusts sending him higher and higher. Then Dillon shifted, tugged him so his ass was hanging right off the table and that long prick pushed right into his gland.

"Dillon!" His eyes rolled, heart pounding in his chest. "Again. Fuck. Right there."

"Here?" Dillon nailed it again, a deep, husky sound that might have been a laugh, might have been a desperate moan coming from the man.

The table was rocking hard now, with each thrust, dishes clacking together, sweat beginning to bead up over Dillon's skin. The scent of the two of them took over. The coil of need in his belly let go with a snap, his cry bitten out as he shot, heat covering his belly.

"Oh, fuck!" Dillon's cock froze deep within him while his body clamped down hard. Then, as soon as his body'd relaxed a little, Dillon started pumping again, the thrusts hard and sure, driving that thick prick into him over and over again.

"Almost... there. Just... Oh!" Dillon cried out and pushed in one last time, hips pushing in tiny pulses. Then Dillon stilled, gasping for air, grinning down at him.

"Hey." He grinned right back, back sticking on the table as the sweat dried.

Dillon leaned into him, reached over and grabbed a chunk of pineapple from above his head. The fruit glided across his lips, then Dillon leaned in and licked the juices away. Then the fruit returned to his mouth.

"Mmm..." He nibbled and sucked on the sweet-tart flesh, humming over the flavor.

Dillon groaned, the prick inside him jerking. "Baby, your mouth is made for sin." Dillon's lips pressed against his, tongue pushing in, sliding over his teeth and gums.

Dal sucked on Dillon's tongue a bit, enjoying the flavors of fruit and man and sex. Dillon groaned into the kiss as his prick slid out, then he bit at Dal's lower lip and slowly stood back, hands taking his and tugging him back up into a sitting position. "What do you think about filling a plate with some more goodies off the table and I'll show you the bedroom?"

"Works for me." He focused on sweet rather than savory, nibbling on this and that to make sure it was to his liking. Berries and tiny tarts, sugared grapes, dark chocolate -- mmm.

Dillon seemed content to leave him to it,

those dark eyes watching him. Every now and then Dillon would grab his hand and eat from his fingers, eyes holding his as the warm, wicked tongue licked over his skin. He just went with it, making sure to get his fingers sticky with honey as he grabbed some baklava.

Dillon all but purred, hand taking his wrist and raising his fingers to Dillon's mouth. The strong body was warm and solid as Dillon rubbed against him, almost idly. One sweet moan followed another, Dillon's tongue sliding on his skin before Dillon sucked his fingers right in, going down on them one at a time.

"Mmm. Bed. Bed, Dillon." He was melting. Honestly. Balls to bones.

"I like the way you think." Dillon gave him a wink and took his hand, leading him back out toward the front hall. "The bedrooms are on the other side of the house. There's a couple of small guest rooms that are never used and then the master bedroom." Dillon waggled his eyebrows at Dal. "The fully stocked master bedroom."

Dillon didn't give him time to really look around; he only had an impression of luxury and beauty, and then they were in the room at the far end of the hall.

It was large, dominated by a king-sized bed with navy covers. The walls were a dark red with navy trim, heavy, masculine curtains covering a long window that looked out over the water, which he could just see in the moonlight. There was a heavy wardrobe with matching dresser, along with a low divan in front of a full length mirror.

"Welcome to my parlor," Dillon murmured in his ear.

"I approve." He did, honestly. His bedroom was done in navies and tans, but the red made things spark.

"We can explore everything tomorrow. Play, fuck, make each other scream. For now..." Dillon led him to the bed, took the plate from him and sat it on the heavy bedside table that matched the armoire and dresser. The covers were pulled back, the sheets cream and soft looking. "You look like you're ready for bed."

"Oh..." God, yes. He swayed a little and then crawled into the bed, body heavy. Exhausted. God.

Dillon left him only long enough to turn the light off and then joined him, pulling him against the warmth of Dillon's body and covering them both with the sheets and comforter. "Sleep," whispered Dillon. "You're mine for the next two weeks, and you're going to need your strength."

"Yeah. Yes. Two weeks." Heaven. Pure heaven.

Chapter Four

Dillon could hear the waves on the beach, and his arms were full, Dal's lovely body plastered against his. It was a dream he'd had often since their encounter at his private resort and he tried to hold onto it as long as possible. Soon the alarm would ring and he'd have to start yet another long, tedious day. Fuck, he needed a holiday.

No, what he needed was a good, hard fuck with a lovely man in a tight corset, nipples rouged, eyes kohled... He still resented Doug Pepper for crapping out on that deal and leaving him picking up the damned pieces and canceling his plans with Dal.

Damn it, he was getting ticked now and waking up and... oh.

Right.

The beach house *with* Dal. And not a dream. He relaxed, sliding a little, rubbing against Dal's lovely body. No wonder his prick was so hard.

Dal groaned, still sound asleep, dark hair tousled and mussed. So pretty. So lovely. And this time in *his* bed. There was a bruise on Dal's throat, fresh and dark. His.

He chuckled. Fuck, what was it about Dal that made him so fucking possessive. Maybe it was the fact that he knew this about Dal, that he knew what the man needed, deep down inside, what Dal hid from the world. He slid his fingers over the bruise, pressing lightly.

That earned him a deep, sweet sound as Dal stretched, hips canting. "Dillon."

"Oh, yeah, baby, it's me." Fuck, he loved that sensuality. Hard to believe that a hedonist like Dal could hide himself away behind contacts and suits and a prim, butter-wouldn't-melt-in-his-mouth manner. He nuzzled Dal's neck, fingers sliding on the smooth skin, skating downward.

"Mmmhmm." Dal turned to face him, eyes slowly opening, giving him a look at those light, bright eyes.

Heat spread through his belly, making him groan. Oh yeah, look at those eyes, bare and true, real. For him. His fingers slid over Dal's features, the man's whiskers scratching his fingertips. "Morning."

"Mmmhmm. Did we sleep long?"

"The sun is up. Has been a while, I imagine." It didn't really matter. They had two whole weeks. Fourteen days to enjoy the pleasure of each other's company. He'd called his secretary Nancy and told her to rearrange his schedule; he was taking his holidays now.

He licked at Dal's earlobe, mouth nipping the very bottom of it, waking the nerves there. His fingers trailed along Dal's belly, the muscles shifting beneath his fingertips.

Dal groaned, stretched for him, so long and lean and fine. "What a wonderful way to wake up."

He admired the lean length, let his fingers trail over Dal's hips and thighs, then dragged his fingers back up again. "It is. It was a pretty good way to go to sleep, too." He blew into Dal's ear and then nibbled at the lovely jaw.

"Flattery will get you laid." Dal laughed for him, the sound deep and husky, pure sex.

He hummed, rubbing lazily against Dal, his prick dragging over that beautiful skin. "Getting laid is definitely in my plans."

He turned Dal's face, pressing their mouths together, moaning into the kiss. Dal wrapped around him, bringing them together shoulders to knees. His hands slid to Dal's ass, squeezing it, sliding Dal up an inch or two and then back down. Their pricks slid together, hot, hard, silky. They were like brands against his belly, burning so good.

His tongue explored Dal's mouth, the kiss not hard yet, not urgent. As if they had all the time in the world. It felt easy, like they had been doing this for months, for years. Dal tasted sweet and warm, tasted like heaven. His hand slid along Dal's back, sliding over the long spine, cupping and stroking Dal's shoulder blades. Every curve was sexy as hell and he touched as much as he could. They ended up twisted in the sheets, chuckling into the kisses, Dal's eyes dancing.

"Your skin is softer than my sheets." And felt so good to rub against, to touch, to lick, to bruise and bite.

"And think, I don't even moisturize." The sparks of humor still surprised him, still shocked

Secrets, Skin and Leather

him. He chuckled, surprised as well by how much he enjoyed laughing with this man. It was like he was more alive with Dal.

"Good thing," he murmured. "Or you'd taste and smell like something creamy instead of..." His nose slid along Dal's throat, the scent there strong, all male. "Like pleasure."

"And here I thought part of the idea was to get all creamy..." Dal lifted his chin, throat working, offering him more skin.

His breath left him in another rush of laughter. "But I want that bitter salt *male* cream, not coconut or flowers or anything... fruity." He eyed the long line of Dal's throat, picked his spot and wrapped his lips around warm skin.

"Mmm." Dal's fingers slid into his hair, tightening, holding him there. Oh, someone liked that, liked it a lot.

His teeth dragged over Dal's skin, and he sucked strongly, pulling Dal's flavor into his mouth. His hips worked, pushing his cock along Dal's belly in time. Dal started pushing as well, the friction slip-sliding from easy and sweet to hard and needy. He hummed around Dal's throat, vibrating the skin in his mouth, one hand pushing between them to find and pinch one of Dal's nipples.

Dal groaned and chuckled, arching under him. "Damn. You... That... Uhn."

"Uh-huh. Always right there, isn't it?" He groaned, mouth moving to the nipple he'd pinched, teeth biting at it. His hips worked harder, the velvet heat of Dal's cock like a sweet brand against his belly.

"Uh-huh. Right there." Dal rolled, humping against him like a desperate puppy.

He bit down hard on Dal's nipple, pressing harder, fingers digging into Dal's ass he tugged them together. Heat sprayed up over his belly, wet and thick, the scent of sex heady.

"Yes." He humped hard, thrusting against Dal, his prick sliding slickly through Dal's come. He gasped as he shot hard, adding to the slick heat between them.

"Mmm. Morning." Dal chuckled, rubbed their noses together. "That wasn't bad at all."

"No, not bad at all." He licked Dal's lips and rubbed a little, their bodies sliding slickly. "Now we could go wash this mess off in the shower, or we could just wipe off and go walk on the beach. I want to show you my ocean," he admitted.

"Oh, then a hot shower and coffee before we bundle up and wander."

Dal smiled up at him. "You think we'll get any snow while I'm here?"

He laughed and shook his head. "Not 'til closer to Christmas. We can come back then and play in it. Make snow angels." His own words made him stop a moment. Plans. He was making plans for something more than a month away. With a lover.

He cleared his throat and got up, sliding out bed and shivering as the covers slid away. "Come on, let's get that shower."

"Right behind you." Warm hands landed on his ass, squeezing and rubbing.

The contrast between the warmth of Dal's hands and his body and the cold hardwood flooring made Dillon shiver again and he hurried to the master bathroom. The room was done in greens, like a forest, and he touched the thermostat to make the heat come on and warm the tile, which was colder underfoot than the hardwood had been.

"Mmm. Hurry, hurry. Hot water before we freeze!" Dal was bouncing and laughing, rubbing against his back.

He would have turned and taken Dal into his arms, teased the man, but he was cold enough his balls were trying to get back into his body -- he'd forgotten how cold New England could be in November -- and he turned on the hot water, growling a little as it took its sweet time warming up. "Give it a minute," he said, pushing back into Dal's warmth.

"In a minute, we'll be queercicles."

"Queercicles... oh, fuck, Dal." He started laughing, leaned against the tile and the sound turned into a yelp. "Yeah, we will actually. Come *on*!" He turned the hot tap on higher and, thank God, there was the hot water. He got it adjusted just right and went in, pulling Dal along with him. "No melting away now."

"I swear. I'm not made of sugar." Dal stretched out, humming low as the steam rose.

"No, you've the kick of spice to you." He leaned back against the water-warmed tile, hand reaching out to slide over Dal's skin. Fuck, the man was sexy. The thought kept hitting him in the balls, making them ache just a little with his need to touch and fuck and make the lovely skin his own. Fuck, he couldn't remember the last time he'd been this taken with anyone. Anyone. Ever.

Dal grinned and reached up, spine crackling and popping. "Man, that water feels good."

"So fucking sensual." He circled Dal's navel, then lower, sliding his fingers along the sweet dips by Dal's hips.

"Is there anything you don't like? Don't enjoy? Don't throw yourself into?"

"Religion. Politics." Dal winked. "Falling interest rates."

"Ah, the boring things. Like three-piece suits and brown contacts." He reached for the soap, slowly slicking up his hands, eyes wandering, deciding where he'd start.

"Depends on what the three pieces are. Some aren't so bad." Oh, that was a wicked look.

It made him catch his breath and, when he released it, a little moan sounded. "You have experience with the good ones, do you?" It was a good thing he didn't want to play it cool, because he couldn't, not when every movements, every word, every look from Dal revved him right up. He slid his soapy finger across Dal's right nipple.

Dal stretched farther, enjoying him. "Nice hands."

Nodding, he slid across to flick at Dal's other nipple, and then wrapped his hands around Dal's ribs, moving them up and down to soap Dal up. "They're awfully fond of your skin."

Dal stole the soap from him, quick as you please, and started lathering him up, hands pushing into the muscles of his arms and chest.

"Fuck, I love the way you touch me." He reveled in it, in fact. Most guys he fucked, he played with, they wanted to be done to, to have him bite and lick and plug. Nobody touched him, not like Dal did.

"Mmmhmm." Dal focused on what he was doing. There wasn't even an attempt to arouse, to get him up again. Dal was just *touching* him.

And he touched back, watching the way Dal the whole time, losing himself in being the focus of the those bright blue eyes. He was lathered and scrubbed, then rinsed. Dal washed his hair, fingernails scrubbing his scalp lightly, sensitizing his skin.

His eyes closed and he moaned, just melting against the tiles. "Jesus, baby, you're good at that."

"Everybody needs a talent."

A brief kiss brushed his shoulder.

He chuckled, his own fingers sliding, wandering. He wasn't even making a pretence anymore that he was washing Dal. He was just enjoying himself. His fingers carded through the curls around Dal's cock. "Gonna let me shave this off and see, baby? I could do it right now."

Dal shook his head. "No, I don't think so."

"No?" He raised an eyebrow. Dal was denying him? But he wanted to see. He pouted. "We have two weeks."

"Are you saying you can't fill two weeks up

just like that with other stuff?" Oh, now that was a challenge and Dillon couldn't resist. Especially from Dal.

"You know I can. You'll see. I'm gonna do things to you you've never even thought of."

Dal rippled and moaned for him, pressing close and resting against him as the water rained down on them, hot and good, wrapping them in their own world. They stayed like that until the temperature changed, just the smallest bit, but enough to notice.

"We've got about another five minutes of hot water," he warned.

"Then we should get dry and bundled up. You promised me a walk on the beach."

"I did. It's a lovely beach, too. Sand, waves, fresh air." He leaned into Dal as he reached to turn off the water.

"Sounds perfect." Dal's lips brushed against his, the kiss surprisingly sweet.

Humming, he kept their lips pressed together, skin gliding on skin, his tongue licking for a moment before their lips parted. He grabbed one of the fluffy bath towels, wrapping it around Dal's shoulders before grabbing one for himself. This sharing thing, himself, his favorite things, a shower that didn't involve sex, it was all new. It was kind of nice.

"Mmm. Cozy." Dal wandered over to the sink. "I don't suppose you have a toothbrush that's new?"

"There should be several in the cupboard under the sink. The staff keeps me well stocked,

Secrets, Skin and Leather

as they never know when to expect me. There should be toothpaste, combs, soap. A razor." He grinned at Dal's look. "For your face. There'll be underwear, sweats, T-shirt in the dressers. All in my size, of course, but I imagine they'll keep you warm while we're outside." He grinned lazily. "And you won't need clothes inside."

"You don't think? I might be easily chilled..." He did love that little tease.

He pulled Dal close, rubbing the towel over the sweetest skin in the world. "I'll make sure that doesn't happen, baby. You're not going to have a chance to get chilled while I'm around."

"Mmm... You're going to spoil me."

He nodded. "I just might." After all, he was getting off on doing it.

He traced a nipple, watching the combination of his finger and the air harden the little nub of flesh. So responsive, sensitive -- was there any wonder he was so damned fascinated?

"Come on. Walking. Wa-a-a-a-alking." Dal laughed -- not at him, just with pure, infectious happiness.

He joined in and they were still laughing as he pulled out a couple pairs of sweatpants and sweatshirts. "I love these," he told Dal, taking the man's hand and sliding it along the inside. "So soft, good against the skin."

"Oh..." Dal actually shivered. "Oh, those are something."

"Warm and soft, could you ask for anything more?" Bending, Dillon opened the bottom drawer and pulled out one of the corsets he'd bought in anticipation of the trip that had never happened all those weeks ago. "Unless it was to ask you to wear this and only this beneath."

It was an emerald green, wonderful soft leather with a pattern raised almost like suede running through it. It would begin just below Dal's nipples and end on his hips, would squeeze the trim waist in tight. He'd had such fun shopping after their encounter at the resort and he'd masturbated one night with this particular corset held to his face, each breath drawing the scent of the leather into his nose, his lungs.

"Oh, love..." The sweats were dropped, Dal's fingers dragging along the leather. The long, thin cock started to fill, to rise.

Dillon licked his lips and took a breath, breathing in leather and soap and the beginning of Dal's need. "I've been picturing you in it at the most inappropriate times." His own fingers slid over the leather, over Dal's hands. "I'll help you put it on."

Dal nodded, eyes heated. "It's sexy as fuck. Where do you want me?"

"Why don't you just lean over the dresser. That way you can brace your hands and watch in the mirror at the same time." And that way he could see both the back and front views.

"Mmmhmm." Dal offered him a soft kiss, then that amazing ass bent over the dresser, thighs spread just so. That sweet, tight ass pushed out at him as Dal leaned, the pale skin begging for his touch, his tongue, his attention.

Oh, fuck. It made him want, the way Dal gave

Secrets, Skin and Leather

himself up like that, just offered himself over to Dillon as easy as you please. Moaning, he slid his hands over Dal's ass, the silk so good under his fingers. "So lovely, baby."

He took a breath and steadied himself, ignored the way his cock rose, the way his balls throbbed. He had to, or he was never going to survive the next two weeks. It would be a Hell of a way to go through. Besides, he'd promised to keep Dal busy.

He kissed Dal's spine and then slid the leather around Dal's chest, positioning the top just below Dal's sweet nipples. His hands weren't shaking as he wrapped the emerald corset around Dal's body, but it was a near thing. He threaded the strong, leather tie through the top holes and pulled the top edges of the corset together.

"Does it fit?" Did it fit -- the leather enveloped Dal like a glove, caressing and cradling and squeezing that fine body.

"You tell me," he murmured, voice husky. He slid his hands along Dal's sides, from the top through to the bottom of the corset, the tight leather pulling Dal's waist in, not as tight as a cincher might, but tight enough. He watched in the mirror, his hands moving on the leather, on Dal's skin like the very best pornography a man could find.

"Tighten the laces, love. Make me feel it." Demanding man. Of course, he gave into those demands so readily, did he not?

With a hum, he began at the top and slowly worked his way down, a scant quarter inch of slack near the top becoming almost a foot by the time he reached the bottom, Dal's breathing coming quick and shallow. He spread the ties out over the lovely buttocks. Stunning. Absolutely stunning. "Better?"

"Tight. Fuck."

He could see in the mirror that he'd positioned it right, the front top of the lovely garment stopped just below Dal's nipples, drawing his eyes to the small, dark coins of flesh. Still, he slid his fingers along the top edge to the front, flicking first one, and then the other nipple. Meeting Dal's eyes in the mirror, he murmured, "Perfect."

"I keep thinking about putting rings in, but they'd show in a business shirt."

A shudder moved through him. "They would." It was a shame, because just the thought of two silver rings in the tight, hard nipples had the heat in his belly growing.

He reached between Dal's legs, fingers finding the rings buried there, tugging them, twisting them. "They would and that will not do. The rings are for my eyes only." He reached further between Dal's legs to see if the man was hard. Oh, yes. Hard and wet-tipped and hot. "I believe I have a cock-ring that matches the corset." He stroked Dal's prick a few times, thumb sliding through the liquid at the tip, pushing into the slit just a little. "It's in the top drawer, right-hand side."

Dal reached and fumbled, fingers searching over plugs and clamps, oil and cream and...

Secrets, Skin and Leather

There. Excellent.

"Yes, that's it. Beautiful, isn't it? And just like the corset, it'll look even better on you." He licked along the top of Dal's corset, focusing on where Dal's spine disappeared beneath the emerald leather. "Put it on, but remember that I'm watching."

"That means what, exactly?" Dal reached down, slowly jacking his cock.

He moaned softly. "That I want a show. Just like that."

Dal spread, fingers moving, sliding the slick wetness along that long shaft.

"I want a show, but no coming," he warned, the scent wafting up from Dal's cock and making his own prick jerk.

"What will you do if I can't wait?" Hips rolling, Dal just pushed and pushed.

"That's what the ring is for, baby. Now work it on nice and slowly." He pushed up against Dal's ass, letting his prick slide along Dal's hot crack.

Dal moaned, the leather slipped around the base of his cock and around those tight, heavy balls. The moan he got as the leather fastened was sweet as fuck. So damned beautiful. So damned sexy.

He kept rubbing against Dal's crack, looking at the stunning picture Dal made in the mirror. "Look," he said softly, pointing to the mirror. "Look at how your prick and your nipples have gone the same dark red over emerald leather. Look at how they're both hard and needy, begging for my touch." He bit at Dal's shoulder, rubbing harder, the tip of his prick bumping against Dal's tailbone again and again, the sensation maddeningly good.

Those blue eyes danced for him, Dal young and wanton and so *alive*. "Then touch me, love."

He laughed, groaned as the tip of his prick hit that little bone again. "What about... our walk on the beach?"

"You want me to walk? Like this?"

"I do." Dillon kept rubbing. He wasn't wearing a cock ring and could come when he wanted to. "I want to watch you walking knowing that as soft as the sweats are, your prick is aching as it rubs against them. I want to know that you feel every breath you take." He chuckled. "I could find some clamps for your nipples as well..."

"Not a chance. There's a plug in there. The drawer is shut." Dal grinned, shoved him back away from the dresser.

He laughed, arms going around Dal, tugging that sweet as back hard against his groin. "You're worried I'm going to get more ideas than I already have? I'm not sure that's possible. Think of a perversion and I have dreamed of doing it to you, Dal." He moaned, body sawing against the heat of Dal, the lovely silk of his skin.

"I think you need a ring, too." Dal's fingers circled his cock, squeezed firmly.

Oh, he loved how Dal always pushed, always turned things around. "I would, you know." He looked into Dal's eyes and tried to push his prick through Dal's tight fist. "For you."

"I know. You'll not come until I let you, even without one, too." Dal went down to his knees, licking and lapping at the tip of his cock.

His eyes widened. No one had ever spoken to him like that before. It made him fucking hard, made him ache. Dal's mouth didn't hurt that any either. "Bold," he murmured, fingers moving to slide through Dal's hair.

Dal smiled, lips wrapping around the swollen tip of his cock, tugging and pulling slightly. He groaned, hips jerking. He was ready to come -- wanted to with all that rubbing he'd been doing and the way Dal looked, tied into his corset, on his knees, mouth spread wide. His hips jerked, pushing his cock further into Dal's mouth. Dal opened to him, lips parted, throat taking him in to the root.

"Fuck," he muttered. It was good, too good, too close to making him come, so he pulled out again, which only succeeded in making the pleasure that much more as Dal's red lips clung to his flesh.

He wanted to come, dammit.

Dal's tongue slid along his prick, slowly fucking the tip of his cock. "Baby... Dal." He wasn't going to beg for permission to come.

"Mmmhmm." Those long fingers stroked the skin at the back of his balls.

"Just remember that you're still bound, baby." A little payback could be a lot of fun. For both of them.

Those pretty eyes smiled up at him, lips

swollen around his prick. He groaned, fingers sliding over Dal's cheek, rubbing his thumb across one eyebrow. His hips set up a rhythm, slow as he could stand it -- too quick and he'd be pouring his seed down Dal's throat. Dal's lips clung to his skin, dragging on his flesh and making him shudder. God. He slid his hands behind Dal's head, curling them into fists as he started to really fuck Dal's mouth, his balls just aching. His cock was taken in deep, tight throat squeezing the tip.

"Dal..." It was a warning. He couldn't possibly hold back a moment longer. Not one moment.

Dal's fingers rolled his balls, almost pushing the spunk from him altogether. He cried out, pushing deep and shooting down Dal's throat. He was swallowed down, the heat and pressure perfect, Dal adoring him, worshipping his body. He moaned softly, hands coming back around to stroke the lovely cheeks. "Good, baby. So good."

He tugged on Dal's arm until his cock was released, and Dal stood, dragging that beautiful body along his the whole way. Groaning, he took Dal's mouth, tasting himself there as he pushed his tongue deep. Dal's hands framed his face, fingers stroking his skin, just petting him. He hummed, his own hands sliding along Dal's back, feeling skin and leather and the sweet swells of Dal's ass.

Oh, a man could live for days on those sounds -- deep and rich and happy.

Dal's cock burned like a brand against his

belly, the tip wet where it rubbed against his skin. And the leather had warmed from Dal's skin, the scent of it rising, surrounding him. It was better than anything he could imagine.

"Take me out to see the water." Dal smiled against his lips. "I want to see it with you."

"And I want to show it to you. Share it with you." And when was the last time he'd wanted to share anything with anyone?

"Good. Point me toward the sweats. Something soft on my poor cock."

"This one?" he asked, hand dropping to slide across the tip. "Oh, this isn't a poor cock at all. It's fine. Just fine."

Dal whimpered, arching up into his touch. "That. That's the one."

He hummed, fingers dancing down along the heated flesh until he reached the leather cock ring, circled and pressed against it. "I think you'll find the sweats I'm loaning you adequately soft. Not as soft as my mouth, but soft enough."

"Tease." That pretty prick throbbed and jerked in his hand.

He grinned. "The longer I make you wait, the better it'll be."

He brought their mouths together again, fucking Dal's lips with his tongue before forcing himself to step away from the sexy, warm body.

He tossed a pair of sweatpants and a T-shirt and sweatshirt at Dal. "They'll be a little big on you, but not so much they're falling off."

He pulled out some clothes for himself as well, watching Dal as he got dressed. It was a shame to see that lovely skin covered, but it was worth it to see Dal's lips part as the soft fabric caressed him.

"A nice walk, hot chocolate when we come back. And... then we'll see what needs attention." He chuckled and winked, grabbing Dal's hand and tugging him along.

The air was crisp and cold, the wind biting at them. Dal seemed to love it, though, face turned up toward the ocean spray. The lovely cheeks gained a beautiful color as they walked and walked, talking about nothing in particular. Their hands stayed together, fingers linked, and Dillon was pretty sure he hadn't held hands with a lover since... ever. It didn't matter, though, because it didn't feel ridiculous or hokey. It felt easy and warm and he found himself smiling.

They must have walked for an hour, up and down the beach before he tugged Dal back up toward the house. "You must be freezing. Luckily I know just how to warm you up."

"Do you think so?" Dal leaned toward him, nose cold against his cheek.

"Don't *you* think so?" he asked, turning to blow on Dal's face. It was the closest he'd come to a kiss outdoors. Dal laughed, lips open, close to his. He hummed, looking into the bright eyes. "Inside, baby. You make me need. Especially knowing what you're wearing under those innocuous sweats..."

"Mmmhmm. You promised me hot chocolate and whipped cream." Oh, the things he could accomplish with those on Dal's skin...

He licked his lips and tugged Dal up the veranda and into the house, bringing their mouths together as soon as the door closed behind them. The kiss was hard and deep and long, he hadn't wanted anyone the way he wanted Dal, every little thing turning him on. He tugged on Dal's lower lip as he ended the kiss, fingers pushing the coat off Dal's shoulders. "You'll have your hot chocolate and whipped cream. But I want skin and leather while you have it."

"Spoiled man." Dal scooted in, nose and cheeks red as he began to shiver.

"Me? Spoiled? You're the one getting all the gifts." His lips twitched, and he tugged Dal along into the kitchen. It was warmer there, and if his housekeeper was as good as he was paying her to be, she'd have hot chocolate and whipped cream ready.

It was sitting there with a stack of chocolate-dipped sweets, the cream rich and melting, the steam rising. "Impressive."

Oh, he was going to have to make sure he gave Barbara a huge bonus this Christmas. "Only the best for you, baby."

"Mmm. Do I have to wait?"

"You only have to wait to come. Take off the sweats -- I want to enjoy the view while we play with our food." He picked up a chocolate-dipped strawberry, sliding it across Dal's lips. Dal nibbled, the shoes and sweats sliding off as he nibbled and licked the juices off the berry.

Dillon groaned -- everything about Dal was

an unconscious seduction, from the way he ate and the way he undressed to the way he looked, chest, waist and cock held tight by the lovely green leather. "Yes... just like that."

"Your staff won't come in?" Dal licked the cream off the edge of a mug.

He groaned, eyes on Dal's lips as shook his head. "They're paid to be discreet."

He picked a pretzel, the bottom half of which was covered in dark, dark chocolate. He ran it around one of Dal's dark little nipples, wondering how long he'd have to play before Dal's skin melted the chocolate. It took longer than he imagined; Dal must have been freezing outside, but once it started melting, the scent of chocolate and man was amazing.

He painted around Dal's left nipple, and then the right. He offered the pretzel to Dal, sliding the it between the lovely lips before bending and licking at the chocolate. The chocolate made his tongue drag, those pretty nipples going tight and stiff for him. He flicked his tongue across one and then slid over to the other, wrapping his lips around it and sucking hard. The taste of the chocolate and Dal filled his mouth, the hot musk of man and leather filling his nose.

Oh.

Dal arched, entire body shuddering, fingers digging into his hair. He'd never known anyone as sensuous as Dal, as eager to meet him sensation for sensation, pleasure for pleasure. Groaning, he bit on the tip of the nipple in his mouth, his hand spreading across Dal's belly, feeling the heat coming up through the tightly stretched leather.

"Going to let me come, love?" There was desire in that voice, but no desperation.

"Of course." He pressed against Dal's belly, feeling the heat pouring up from below, Dal's need held at bay, that prick hard and beautiful. He bit at the other nipple and then grinned up at Dal. "Eventually."

"Bitch." Fuck, Dal's laugh made him ache.

His own chuckle was husky, caught somewhere deep in his belly, in his balls. "You love every second I don't let you come. You can feel your heartbeat in your prick, your balls ache, and you feel your need with every breath you take. It's sexy as Hell."

"You think you know me so well?" Dal leaned, licking and lapping at his lips, those blue eyes heated.

"I don't think it -- I know it." He went down onto his knees, reaching for one of the mugs of chocolate. "It's why you came."

He took a sip of chocolate, holding it in his mouth a moment before swallowing it and then swallowing down Dal's prick.

"Dillon!" Dal's scream rang out, hands slapping down on the counter.

A shudder moved through him, his prick jerking in his sweats. Humming, he let his tongue slide around Dal's cock, taking it in further and further as his fingers moved to touch the leather cock ring.

"Let me. Fuck. I need it. Damn." Dal's head

shook from side-to-side.

He pulled off Dal's prick and grinned up. "Patience, baby. Patience." His fingers manipulated those sweet, heated balls.

"Pa...patience?" Dal went up on tip-toe.

"Uh-huh." He placed a kiss on the tip of Dal's prick, licked at the slit. "You haven't touched your hot chocolate," he pointed out, eyes flicking back up to meet Dal's again.

"I... I licked the whipped cream..."

"Whipped cream. Mmm... was it good? Have you tried the chocolate? Barbara makes it from actual chocolate, you know. No powder here. It's rich and dark and sinful." He nipped at the side of Dal's prick, fingers teasing around the leather holding it and Dal's balls captive. Soon, it would have to be soon because his own patience was running thin.

"I'm a fan of sin." Dal spread a little wider, ass begging for him, ring right there.

He pushed his nose between Dal's legs, the scent of the man strong, going straight to his cock. Groaning, he slid his tongue through the little bits of metal. Back and forth, he slid his tongue, the heat of Dal's skin amazing.

He heard Dal drinking, then a deep moan filled the air. "Oh. Fuck. You're better than the chocolate."

He grinned fiercely, taking both rings between his teeth and tugging on them, hands manipulating Dal's balls, the long, sweet cock. Christ, he could lose himself in Dal's heat and scent and need. He shifted again, taking the long, sweet cock into his mouth as he released the rings.

"More..." Dal reached for the cock-ring, hips pushing that cock deep into his throat. Greedy, beautiful man.

He sucked harder, head bobbing as he slapped Dal's hand away and twisted the sweet rings imbedded in that secret patch of skin again.

"Need!" Dal bowed beneath him, fingers gripping the edge of the counter.

He sucked harder, pushing a finger into Dal's body as he tugged on the cock ring. He would have Dal's seed, and he would have it now. Time for patience was over. Not even the leather could hold Dal back, that lovely cock jerking, throbbing as seed splashed against the back of his throat. He swallowed it all down, the sharp salty taste better than any chocolate.

He licked and cleaned Dal's prick before slowly letting it slip from his mouth, leaving the cock ring where it was so Dal would stay hard. Groaning, he rubbed his cheek against the leather on Dal's belly.

Dal whimpered, legs shaking. "Love."

He grinned, pushing up along Dal's body, holding him up against the counter. "I want you, Dal." He nudged his cock against Dal, growling at the sweatpants in the way -- soft as they were, they weren't Dal's skin.

"Then take me. I'm right here, Dillon." Dal turned, leaned over the counter, ass offered over.

Dillon moaned, tugging his sweats down, his prick pushing out eagerly. His prick slid along

Dal's crack. So fucking good -- he wanted in. Dal's hips rolled, ass humping the air, tempting him. Begging him. He reached over to nearest drawer, searching for some lube and a condom. He came up empty and growled, tugging open the next one. There *had* to be something in here. He did find condoms, but no damned lube.

"You're not shoving a turkey baster up there."

He started to laugh, leaning his head against Dal's back. "Are you sure?" he asked. "What if it's the only option?"

"Then you're out of luck. No. Turkey. Basters." Dal laughed, head tossing, body bouncing with each chuckle.

Grinning, he slid his hands down along Dal's sides, the leather rough against his fingertips, especially in comparison to Dal's skin. "How about my tongue?" he asked, going to his knees and rubbing his face against Dal's ass.

"Mmm." Oh, it appeared that Dal approved. Wholeheartedly.

Humming, he spread Dal's ass cheeks, held the corset ties to the side, and licked along Dal's crack. Once, and then again, and then he pressed the point of his tongue inside Dal's hole.

"Oh, fuck. Yeah, love. So hot."

He moaned his agreement. Dal was all heat and silk inside, and Dillon pressed in closer, pushed his tongue deeper. Dal leaned down, spreading for him, asking for more without saying a word. And he gave it, tongue pushing into Dal, fucking that little hole over and over again. He spread Dal further, thumbs teasing

Secrets, Skin and Leather

their way in, stretching Dal.

Dal gave it up for him, rocking and pushing and begging him. Begging him for more. Yeah, that was it, Dal so fucking sensuous, it made his head spin. He thrust his tongue deeper, making Dal good and wet. He finally stopped tongue-fucking Dal, moving between Dal's legs to tongue the sweet little rings. He pushed three fingers into Dal, making sure his lover was well stretched.

Dal grunted, pushing down and taking his fingers, the deep cry ringing out. His Dal was beautiful, and he could just picture that amazing ass with his entire hand buried in it. Just the thought had him jerking, his teeth tugging hard on both rings.

"Dillon! Love!" Dal jerked, body shuddering above him.

He tugged hard again and then rose up behind Dal, his fingers sliding out of the tight heat. "You ready for this, baby? Ready to be taken?"

"No teasing. Give it to me."

"So pushy, baby. I have a half a mind to make you wait until this evening." Of course that would mean he had to wait too, and that was most definitely not going to happen. He was already opening the condom.

"You won't wait." Dal arched, ass rubbing against him.

He let his prick rub along Dal's crack, biting back his moan as the way was slickened by the drops of heat sliding from his tip. "You sound awfully sure for a man who wants to get fucked as badly as you do."

"I'm sure. You may make me pay for it later, but I'm sure now." Such a pushy, bratty bottom. Dillon loved it.

He didn't answer, just pushed the head of his cock past the tight ring of muscles, holding there for an excruciating count of three before sinking all the way in. Dal rippled, hands sliding on the counter as the man stretched and rocked.

"Fuck. Oh, baby." God, he'd never felt anything like being buried in the tight, grasping heat of Dal's ass. Never.

His hands wrapped around Dal's hips, just below the bottom of the corset, his fingers gripping hard enough he knew he'd leave bruises. Just the thought made it that much hotter and his hips jerked, pushing him in as deep as he could go.

"Yeah. Need." They found their rhythm, slamming and slapping together, eyes rolling, cries pouring from Dal.

He pounded into Dal until he was on the verge of coming, until he couldn't possibly hold it back much longer. Reaching around Dal, he flicked open the cock ring and wrapped his hand around Dal's prick, tugging it sharply. "You can come now," he told Dal. "Let me feel you on my cock."

"Love..." He felt Dal's orgasm, all the way around his cock before heat sprayed on his fingers.

He rode it out, teeth sinking into Dal's shoulder as his body shuddered, sheer will keeping him from coming. Once Dal had stilled, panting, trembling, he jerked in a few more times, letting himself go. It was fucking sweet, the pleasure long and slow and all over.

Groaning, he collapsed against Dal's warmth, one hand shooting out to hold onto the counter, elbow locking. "Baby..." He licked at the mark on Dal's shoulder -- a perfect impression of his teeth.

"Uh-huh." Dal nodded, slumping a little. "Damn."

"Yeah." He nuzzled Dal's shoulders and neck for a moment, but it was too cool to hang around naked for long, especially with their skin damp with sweat. With a last, lingering lick to Dal's nape, he pulled out. Their groans matched, Dal's body seeming to hold on, to squeeze him tight and beg him to stay.

He got Dal turned around, propped up against the counter to take a long, lingering kiss as he disposed of the condom.

"Mmm." Dal pushed close, the heat difference between leather and skin distracting him. His hands traced over Dal's spine, traveling from skin to leather and back to skin again. One kiss melted into another and then another, until finally he pulled away, Dal such an addiction.

"So what did you think of my beach?" he asked, rubbing their noses together.

"It's cold. Beautiful. I can see why you have a home here."

He nodded, looked around the kitchen, out the window at the beach and the steel grey sky. "I'm not here often," he admitted. But it made a lovely destination when he needed to get away. "I've never brought anyone here before."

"No?" Dal leaned back into him. "I've never been with someone more than once."

So they were both stepping out of their comfort zone. It mollified that voice inside his head that had screamed at him for admitting Dal was the only person he'd brought here. "Well then, I suppose we'll have to see what other firsts we can manage, hmm?" He chuckled, arms wrapping tighter around Dal. "I have a hunch it won't be an easy task."

"Are you saying we're not easy?" Dal's laugh was deep, sexy. Sweet.

He goosed Dal for that. The squeak he got was fucking fine.

"The only one you better be easy with these days is me, baby." The words were out before he could stop them.

Dal looked at him, straight on and still. "You think that you can keep me busy, lover?"

"I do. I think I can keep you busy enough you can hardly catch your breath. And if I can't, I can always tie you to the bed..."

"Promises, promises." Dal framed his face, tongue sliding on his lips.

He hummed, tongue pushing out to lick at Dal's, but not deepening the kiss, letting Dal lead. "I have cuffs in my bedroom."

"You have all sorts of lovely toys and you have me." Dal smiled against his lips.

"What more could I want?"

And just at this very moment he couldn't think of a single thing.

Chapter Five

There was snow falling, slow and steady, and Dal was dozing on the sofa, mulled wine making the room smell wonderful. Dillon had turned him inside out and rightside in and Christ.

He was ruined.

For life.

Still, it was a glorious thing.

"Don't you look about as decadent as anyone can," murmured Dillon, voice at his ear, followed by a soft lick to his earlobe. "Seeing you lying there in sweats, knowing what's underneath despite the innocent sprawl..." Dillon hummed. "Gives me ideas, baby."

"Mmm." Like Dillon needed ideas. "Are you thinking of the great American novel?"

Dillon laughed softly, and one finger slid over the heavy, dark mark on his neck. "Not exactly."

His eyelids drooped, the zing inside him just maddening. "No?"

Dillon's hum was satisfied, and his finger pressed the mark a little harder. "No, I'm thinking of the great American pastime."

"Bowling?"

Dillon moved to lie on him, weight good, heavy. That talented tongue slid across his lower lip. "Nope. More body contact than bowling."

"You feel fucking good, man." He reached up, lapping at Dillon.

Dillon gave a slow smile that lit up his face. "Yeah, that's the idea. And you? Feel amazing. I want to keep feeling you until I know every fucking inch by heart."

Oh. Oh, man. That made his cheeks heat, made a mixture of pleasure and passion and a little worry fill him.

"Mmm, that's a lovely look, baby. All flushed, wanton and wanting." Dillon wriggled on him, the man's prick hard against his thigh.

"You're something else." Something more than he'd ever expected. Dillon grinned down at him, the look cocky. But Dillon's pleasure at his words showed in the blue eyes.

He stretched out, eyes caught by the snow. God, it was all beautiful.

Dillon was busy licking and nibbling at his neck, taking total advantage of his stretch. "What's got your attention, baby?"

"It's just good, here. The snow, the warm, you."

"I want to make it better. I want to give you something you'll never forget." Dillon's voice had dropped, grown husky.

"Mmm." He could handle better.

"I'll never forget it either, baby. Holding you in my hand..."

"Hmm?" Dal reached for a kiss, lips parted, hungry.

Dillon gave it to him, mouth devouring his. As their lips parted, Dillon whispered. "Come to bed, we can't do this on the couch."

He was obviously missing something, but it

didn't really matter, because those heated eyes promised pleasure.

Dillon stood, the motions graceful, and held out a hand to him. "You need anything, baby? I don't want to be interrupted once we start -- we'd lose the flow of it building."

"No. Just you. Just need you."

"All right. Shower first, yeah? We'll make you clean. Inside and out, baby." Dillon's fingers curled warmly around his, leading him back into the large bathroom where he'd already come more times than he could remember. Dillon turned absolutely everything into a sexy, exciting experience from washing to eating to brushing their teeth...

God, the man had made him wear a plug and had played with it while he practically fellated the toothbrush, cock sliding against the cold porcelain of the sink... He turned toward Dillon, lips exploring the long column of that tanned throat, nipping as he let the memory wash over him, make him hard. Dillon moaned for him, head going back, giving him the long line of neck to work with as they stopped just inside the bathroom door. Warm, sure fingers that knew his body more intimately now than anyone ever had slid beneath his sweatshirt and slowly teased it upward.

He nibbled the throbbing vein there, chuckling as Dillon shivered. "Love how fucking sensitive you are." God, he wished time would slow down.

"I think that's my line," murmured Dillon,

fingers teasing around his navel before sliding up further to explore his nipples, both still ultra sensitive after a long bout with a wicked pair of nipple clamps.

He gasped, went up on his toes, pure fire pouring through him. "Dillon. Damn. I... Oh."

Dillon looked like the cat that ate the cream, so pleased with himself.

Thumbs sliding across his nipples one last time, Dillon pulled Dal's sweatshirt right off, leaving him bare to the air's cool touch. His nipples were a dark red, so sensitive they ached, belly tight as a board, one dark love bite by his navel.

"God. Fuck." Dillon's voice was husky and a low, throaty moan came from him. "You're so fucking beautiful. You make me need." Dillon's fingers stroked over the mark by his navel, the other hand moving lightly over the place where his sweatpants tented out.

"Yeah. We're bad as addicts." His cock jumped a little, fighting to get some of Dillon's attention.

"Mmm, but what we're not doing's illegal." Dillon stopped a moment, head tilting. "In most states." He was given a wink, one of Dillon's hands dipping into the sweatpants to slide past his prick and cup his balls.

"Mmm." He rocked into the touch, pushing his piercings against Dillon's fingers.

"So pushy, baby." Dillon's laughter was threaded through his voice, little finger sliding through both rings and tugging.

"Uh-huh. You love it." Goddamn. Just. God. Damn.

He got a grin, Dillon's eyes so hot, and just eating him up as his piercings were tugged again, twisted a little. "And you're going to love what's coming, so get me naked, baby, and we'll start off in the shower."

"Mmm." Dal took his time, enjoying the touches and the kisses. He got off on touching the man, sliding his hands down Dillon's arms, Dillon's sides.

His touches earned hums and moans, Dillon as sensual as the man kept accusing him of being.

"Shower, baby." So focused today.

"Okay. Okay. Do I smell bad?" He winked and turned toward the faucets, turning it to hot.

Dillon laughed and shook his head. "No, but I'm not in the mood to get distracted from this."

"You're not going to try to shave me again, are you?" He knew Dillon was curious, knew Dillon wanted to see, but he was holding back, keeping Dillon curious. He wasn't exactly sure why, and if he looked too closely... well, he didn't look too closely.

The water started pouring down, splashing against his skin. Mmm. Hell, yes. Joining him, Dillon's fingers spread soap over his skin, helping the water to wash it immediately away. Again and again, Dillon's fingers returned to his crack, sliding along it with promise. He propped one leg up on the side of the tub, spreading himself a little for that touch, letting Dillon in.

Secrets, Skin and Leather

Oh, that soft sound was sexy, one of Dillon's fingers pushed right into him, opening him up. Dal reached up, grabbed the showerhead and stretched out. Yum.

"Yes, just like that." Dillon's body slid against him, a second finger pushing in with the first.

"Have you done this before?" Dillon asked. "Am I the first?"

"Done what, lover?"

"Had someone's hand inside you."

Oh.

Oh, sweet fuck.

"No." No. He'd never trusted... Did he trust Dillon enough?

"I am the first." A low sound came from Dillon. "Good. I'm going to touch you like no one else ever has. Ever."

"I. Have you? Done it, I mean?"

"Uh-huh. But it wasn't like this." Dillon's lips slid along his neck, hot tongue sliding along his ear. "It wasn't intimate."

"What was it like?" That touch relaxed him, heat flooding him, and not from the water.

Dillon groaned, fingers finding his gland, hitting it hard. "Unbelievable. Doing it with you is going to blow my fucking mind. Yours, too."

"I. Uh." His eyes rolled back in his head, entire body jerking.

"Going to clean you first, Dal. Fill you with warm water and soap. It'll make you ready for my hand, let you really feel it." He could feel Dillon's cock against his ass, hot, hard, sliding.

"You've got this all planned, don't you?" He

wasn't sure how that made him feel.

"I've been thinking about it since I brought you here."

Dal shuddered, head falling forward as his gland was stroked again and again.

A third finger pushed into him, and Dillon's other hand slid around his prick, thumb sliding over the slit. "You wanna come first? It'll relax you for the cleaning."

"Uh. Uh-huh." Fuck, yes. Please. More. Jesus.

Oh, that laugh slid down his spine, making him shiver. "Hedonist."

The hand around his cock gripped him tighter, jerking him slowly. His head fell back, throat working as Dillon pushed him. Dillon's lips closed around skin by his shoulder blade, sucking up yet another mark. Dal jerked and groaned, entire body going tight as his balls drew up tight.

"I can feel that, feel you ready to come." Dillon's fingers twisted, hitting his gland again, hard.

"Yes. Yes. Please. Love." One more touch and he was coming, calling out Dillon's name over and over.

Dillon moaned, hips rubbing that hard prick against his ass. It slipped away as Dillon reached for the stash of condoms they'd left in the soap dish. "Beautiful."

He canted his hips back, offering his ass. Groaning, Dillon pulled out his fingers and shoved his covered cock in its stead. "Oh, fuck yes."

They slammed together, skin slapping, fingers squeezing tight as Dillon fucked him good and hard. "Yeah. Yeah, just like that."

Dillon moaned and grunted, teeth sinking into his shoulder this time. He grunted as Dillon shot, filled him up, hands clenching on the shower head as it pushed his own orgasm out of him. Yeah. Dillon rested heavily against him for a moment, the water hot and good around them. Then, with a groan, Dillon slid his prick away.

"Gonna fill you with the water and soap now," murmured Dillon. "It's a special soap just for this. Not harsh, but it'll clean you out gently."

"You just want me here?" Despite coming, Dal was vibrating, exciting, jonesing on the sensations.

"I do," murmured Dillon, hands moving on him. "Nice and warm, and you'd wind up in here at some point anyway. Don't move."

A kiss was placed on his neck and Dillon stepped away, the water sluicing down fully over his skin now that his lover wasn't plastered up against him. He watched as Dillon search through the cupboard beneath the sink, pulling out some tubing and a small bladder full of liquid. Then Dillon joined him once again under the spray, using the shower to warm the liquid in the bladder.

"You want to hold this until I need it?" Dillon asked, passing it over. "It's got sterile water and that gentle soap I was telling you about in it."

"Okay." He took it, rolling the soft plastic in his fingers. He wasn't sure what to think here, so he just... didn't.

"My fingers first, baby. Just like always. You know how this goes." One of Dillon's fingers pressed back into him, hot and wriggling, giving him something good to focus on.

"Mmmhmm." He wasn't a virgin, wasn't untried, not even close, but...

Dillon's hand.

Damn.

"I could have started you out with a plug," Dillon said softly as a second finger pushed into him, making sure he was still stretched, teasing across his gland and playing inside him. "That big huge purple one would have had you good and ready. But I don't want this to be a breeze, I don't want you all stretched out like that already. I want you to feel every last inch, every last fucking bit of my hand as it goes into you."

"You can use the plug after, when I'm empty and aching." Hell, if he worked it right, he could get Dillon riled up again and they could just fuck.

The sound Dillon made said that he could and they would, just as needy and wanton as he could ask for. "You do have some wicked ideas, baby. Almost as wicked as mine."

Dillon's fingers slid so only the tips were inside him, stretching him open. "The hose now, baby. It should be nice and warm."

He didn't say anything, just handed the stuff back and closed his eyes.

Dillon's fingers slid out of him, and his muscles closed over the rubber end of the hose.

Secrets, Skin and Leather

It didn't hurt, but it wasn't quite right either: not the warmth of Dillon's fingers or cock or tongue, and not a dildo or vibrator either.

"I'm going to fill it slowly, baby."

"I. Do you want me bent over or something?"

One of Dillon's hands slid up along his back, following his spine. "You can hold onto the shower head or lean against the wall -- whichever is more comfortable. Once you're full you'll have to hold it in."

"Then to the pot. I know how that part works." In theory.

"There's a bedpan in the cupboard, if you wanted to stay in the shower."

He could feel the water pouring inside him now, not fast or anything, just slowly filling him up. Dal rested his forehead on his hand, breathing good and slow, just feeling this like he'd felt so much.

"That's it, just relax and let it happen." Dillon hummed, nibbling his neck, one hand holding his ass, the other rubbing circles around his navel. "You're more than halfway there, baby. Just a few minutes more."

The rest went quick, Dillon helping him, encouraging him and soothing him as he shivered, feeling so exposed, so vulnerable. It wasn't until it was over that he felt like he could breathe, wrapped in a towel, in Dillon's arms.

"So sexy, baby. You make me want so many things." Dillon slowly led him into the bedroom, the carpet thick under his toes.

"We've got some time." The shivers were

right at the surface, excited and needy.

"We do. You know I can come up with more things to do than we've got time for, though. But." Dillon stopped and met his eyes, smiling into them, fingers working beneath the towel to touch his skin, encourage the shivers. "Right now nothing else matters but you me and this moment. A moment you're going to remember forever."

"Forever is a very long time, lover."

Dillon made a fist and showed it to him. "Taking my hand is worthy of remembering forever."

It wouldn't fit. "I can't stretch that much, Dillon. You'll tear me." His fingers traced those fingers, those knuckles.

Dillon's mouth met his, lips sliding on his own, the kiss starting soft and growing harder, deeper. Leaving him breathless.

"I want you to feel it, baby -- I don't want to hurt you." Dillon's eyes held his as the hand beneath his own turned and twined their fingers together. "You'll love it."

Dal lifted his face for a kiss, squeezing Dillon's hand tight. If he didn't, they could stop. The kiss was given, Dillon's mouth hard on his own, the man's breath filling his lungs.

Pushing him onto the bed, Dillon pulled away the towel and came down on top of him, solid and warm. It was fucking easy to stop thinking, stop worrying and just give it up. Rubbing and groaning, hands sliding down Dillon's spine -- fuck yes. Dillon groaned, pushing into him,

Secrets, Skin and Leather

against him, their bodies fitting together just right.

It seemed to take a real effort on Dillon's part to pull away, to move to lie next to him. "I want you on your back, baby. I want to be able to watch your face while I do it."

"Mmmhmm." He moaned, half-turning to one side.

Dillon's hands slid between his legs, encouraged him to let them splay open, exposing himself. "Hard for me again already. That's such a turn on, baby."

"You are something special, man." Something unlike anyone else.

"Mmm. And you're in a category all by yourself, Dal." Dillon's eyes met his and for a moment the world stopped. Just everything stilled and it wasn't about fucking or fisting or anything. It was just them and breathing.

Then it started again, Dillon blinking, eyes flicking down to watch as Dillon cupped his balls, rolled them. He spread so wide his thighs twinged, one knee drawing up so that Dillon could see, could touch.

"Oh, yeah, baby. Just like that." Dillon's hand slipped behind his balls, teased his piercing, stroking his skin. He could feel his skin rippling, the pleasure and tug just perfect. "God, you smell good." Dillon's nose slid along his collarbone, fingers moving further back, sliding along his crack.

"I smell like you, like your soap." Like Dillon's come and shampoo and skin.

"Like I said, good." Dillon gave him a grin and pushed a finger into his ass.

He grinned back, taking Dillon right in, squeezing tight as he rode that touch. Groaning, Dillon fucked him with just that one finger, sliding it in and out. And Dillon kept it up until he thought he was going to scream from just that one finger. So good, but not nearly enough.

"More, lover. Come on." He didn't want to have to beat Dillon with a stick.

"That's what I want to hear," murmured Dillon, slipping a second finger into him. "You're going to beg me for it."

"I don't beg." Oh, better. Much fucking better.

"No? Are you sure?" Dillon's two fingers slid and stretched, twisted inside him.

"Uh. Uh-*huh*." He bucked, toes curling right up. Shit. Right there.

"Love how you respond to every touch, baby." A third finger slipped in, this so familiar from over the last days, so good.

Yeah, well, it felt good. Damn good when Dillon touched him.

In and out, twisting and turning, pegging his gland, coming nearly out and then pushing deep again, Dillon worked him, made him writhe. The sensations flowed and ebbed, made him ache, made him hard and wanting again.

"You want that next finger?" Dillon asked, pinky sliding on his skin around his hole.

"Mmmhmm. Easy. Go easy, lover."

"It's gonna be amazing, baby. Just amazing." Dillon's fingers disappeared, and Dal heard the sound of the tube of slick being opened. A moment later Dillon's fingers were back, were pushing at his hole. He was full, but not hurting, so he didn't bother tensing up. He just took a deep breath, hips rolling so slowly. "Oh, fuck, you're a natural Dal." Dillon's lips slid over his shoulders, all four fingers pushing slowly into him, tips wriggling.

"I. Full of you." His eyes fell closed, all his focus on his ass.

"You are. Not as full as you're going to be though."

Turning, the fingers in him pushed a little deeper and then slid out again. Each movement was slow and smooth.

"I. I don't know if..." Oh. Good...

Dillon hummed, body undulating slowly against him. "Feels good, doesn't it?" One finger slid over his gland, bumping it.

"Good." Fuck. Full. He was supposed to *think*?

"Tell me you want more," murmured Dillon. "Tell me you want it all."

"I." He tossed his head, hands sliding down his belly.

Dillon's lips parted his, tongue pushing in to fuck his mouth a moment or two before sliding away again. "Just one word, baby. Give it to me and I'll be holding you in my hand."

"Please." He wasn't sure whether he was asking Dillon to give him more to stop.

"Anything you want, baby." Dillon's fingers slid away, pushed back in, and then pulled away again. More lube slathered over his hole, Dillon's hand.

"This is it," murmured Dillon, eyes catching his, looking at him, looking *into* him.

He whimpered, nodded. It. He. Damn. Okay.

Dillon curled his hand or something, the tops of those long fingers sliding in pretty easy, and then it started to get thicker, to stretch him out wider than anything he'd ever felt.

"Dillon." Full. *Full.*

"Right here, baby. Right here." The tips of Dillon's fingers wriggled inside him and then stilled again as the push continued. Dillon's eyes were on his face, watching, looking, seeing.

He closed his eyes, tried to focus. Breathe. Get it together.

"Almost there, baby. Inside you."

So wide. So big. There was no way. Just no fucking... oh fuck. Dillon's hand suddenly pushed all the way in. All the way inside him. A deep, overwhelmed cry escaped him, pushed out of him, no room left inside. Dillon held him there, caught on that hand as Dillon's fingers slowly curled into a fist.

"So fucking incredible, baby. So fucking beautiful." Dillon's voice slid over his skin, low and husky, those eyes like a touch on his skin. He fought to catch his breath, entire focus on his ass, the hand spreading him.

"Look, baby," Dillon insisted, nose nuzzling his neck, tongue and lips following, licking a hot line over his skin. "Just look at you, caught on my hand. Fuck." The last word tore from Dillon's mouth with a groan, a shudder going through the strong body pressed against him.

"So full of you. So full." His head tossed, throat working as he tried to wrap his head around what he was feeling.

"Yes. Full of me. Mine. Marking you inside, baby. Where no one's ever touched you before." Dillon sounded possessive, almost growling the words. And then the hand inside him started to move, just slow motions that slid Dillon's knuckles over his gland, rubbing him from the inside.

"In me." He arched, another raw groan tearing from him.

Dillon's free hand slid down over his chest, pushing against his belly and he swore he could almost feel Dillon's hand meeting, touching through him. "In you." The words were reverent, soft and full of wonder.

"Uh-huh." He leaned up, nuzzling into Dillon's shoulder, needing to be close, to feel.

Dillon's free hand kept pushing at his belly for a moment, before sliding down in tandem with the fist inside him and wrapping around his cock. "I don't know which is hotter," murmured Dillon. "Your cock or your ass."

Then his face was nudged, Dillon's mouth closing over his in a long kiss he swore he could feel all the way to his toes. It felt like one orgasm poured over him, then another and another. He wasn't sure what happened, what he really felt, but he couldn't care. All he could do was feel. It went on forever, each movement of either of

Dillon's hands keeping the flow going. Between that and the hard kisses he was breathless, lights dancing behind his eyes. Finally, Dal just melted, allowing himself to breathe and feel, allowing Dillon deep inside.

Dillon's eyes met his, the look full of fierce pleasure and need. "Gonna pull out now, Dal. I want you so badly." Dillon's prick, hard and hot, throbbed against his hip, proof of Dillon's words.

He didn't have any words left; he just nodded.

Okay.

Whatever.

Humming, Dillon kissed him again, tongue sliding over his lips and into his mouth, distracting him from the fact that Dillon's hand was pulling out. At least until the widest part stretched his hole -- so fucking huge. A shudder rocked him, and Dillon's hand stilled. He could feel his own heart beat in the skin stretched around Dillon's hand. Then Dillon's teeth nipped his lower lip, scraping over the skin and Dillon's hand slipped out of him as he gasped.

He actually whimpered, the emptiness inside him huge, almost an ache. Dillon's pressed kisses over his face, soft, hot touches of those lips on his skin. "Sh. Sh, I know. Gonna fuck you now, okay? Gonna ease that need."

Everything inside him reached for those kisses, for his lover. Ease. Please. Yes.

Plastic crinkled and then Dillon's cock pushed against his hole, pressing and then sliding right in. Not as big as Dillon's fist, not by a long shot, it still filled him up, warmed him right through.

Dal hid his face in the curve of Dillon's throat, both of them rocking, sweet and easy. Dillon was right, the sweet glide of that cock inside him eased the ache, fed the fire in his belly, and promised relief for his need. "So good, baby. Fuck."

"Mmmhmm." He wasn't hard, didn't think he'd ever get it up again, but it didn't matter.

Dillon's eyes shone down at him, just looking right at him, right into him. They suddenly widened, Dillon groaning and jerking, heat shooting deep inside him.

Yes. Yes, that was... Yes. He'd lost his words somewhere.

Dillon collapsed down against him with a moan, hands moving idly on his skin. Those fingers seemed to unerringly find the marks Dillon'd left over the last week, stroking some gently, pushing against others.

Yeah. He. Uh. Yeah. "Dillon." He kissed whatever patch of skin was closest, just tasting idly.

He could feel Dillon's grin against his skin. "Now you won't ever forget me."

"No. No, I won't." He couldn't.

"That's right." Dillon's mouth found his, the kiss long and lazy, a hint of heat behind it even as Dillon's prick slid out of him.

As Dillon settled next to Dal, his hands kept moving, always touching. "You look amazing in nothing but pleasure and my marks, baby."

"You spoil me." He was going to hate going back to being Scott.

"Is that a bad thing?" Dillon asked, lips soft on his arm.

"No. No, there's nothing bad here."

"Good."

Dillon sighed and snuggled closer. "Take a nap, baby. I still have a few days left to wear you out."

"Promises, promises." He kissed Dillon's temple, nodded.

"I haven't broken one yet."

"No." He met Dillon's eyes, all sorts of things to say and no words for it. "No, you haven't. You won't."

He knew that.

Knew it balls to bones.

Chapter Six

Dillon checked himself in the mirror. He looked good, the tux fitting him to perfection. It was their last night before they went back to their real lives, and he had a lovely dinner planned for Dal, some dancing. And a night of pleasure.

Dal was in one of the guest rooms, dressing in the clothes he'd left out -- he hoped; with Dal he never knew exactly what he was going to get. It was one of the things he enjoyed about the man. But the white cincher and black silk pants he'd chosen for Dal would look stunning on the man.

His cock stirred just at the thought. Christ, he'd come more in the last two weeks than he had... in the last year. Dal was inspiring.

He glanced over at the clock. Oh, good. Time to meet his lover in the dining room. He turned down the bed first, making sure the drawer in the side table was well equipped. Then he headed out to see what sort of feast had been laid out for them.

Dal was standing, sipping a glass of brandy. The black pants were there, along with a white silk shirt. The shirt just hid the cincher from his sight, teased him with its lines.

"God, you're stunning." Even after two weeks of constantly being together, Dal took his breath away. He'd never known anyone to hold his attention like this.

"I had to make sure to keep your attention." Dal smiled at him, tipped his glass.

"Oh, I assure you, you have it. And not just because we're the only two people here." He winked and reached out for Dal's brandy, turning the glass to drink from the same spot Dal had. He imagined he could taste Dal on the crystal, just a hint of male beneath the burn of the alcohol. From this close, he could see that Dal had rimmed his eyes with a tiny line of black, making the blue pop and shine. He licked his lips, hummed a little. "I hope you're ready for a delightful evening."

"I am. Something to remember on my way to Athens tomorrow."

"Athens. How exciting." He leaned in to nibble at Dal's earlobe. "Forget about tomorrow, baby. You're here with me tonight."

"Yes." Dal nodded, pushed closer, silk sliding against him.

He slid his hand along Dal's shoulder, enjoying the cool silk, the hint of warmth from Dal's skin beneath it. "Come let me feed you. It's my second favorite thing to do."

"Only your second?" Dal chuckled, humoring him, letting him lead.

"It's possibly even further down the list. It depends on whether you count each position as its own item or not." He winked and pulled out a chair for Dal.

"You are deliciously perverted, you know that?" Dal sat, spine straight, posture assured by the leather squeezing him tight.

"I try my best, baby. And I must admit, you do bring the best out of me." He sat in the chair next to Dal, admiring the lines of Dal's body. Dal grinned, those eyes admiring him openly, the look almost physically, certainly enough to make him hard. He couldn't help preening, chest puffing up for Dal, his legs spreading to make room for his cock.

It was going to be an interesting meal.

"Shall we see what we've got here?" he asked, pulling the silver dome off the tray labeled "appetizers."

There was lamb on a stick with sesame seeds, bite-sized pieces of chicken cordon bleu and blue cheese stuffed hamburgers, as well as crab salad in lettuce wraps. All finger foods. He hummed happily.

"You're spoiled rotten." Dal didn't look the slightest bit sorry about it, either. One long-fingered hand reached out, took a lettuce wrap and offered it to him. He didn't deny the charge, just leaned in to take the lettuce wrap from Dal's fingers. His lips closed slowly over the appetizer and Dal's fingers, slowly pulling away. The salt of Dal's skin seasoned the lettuce wrap perfectly. Sitting back, he moaned softly as he chewed, the flavors full and rich in his mouth.

"That must taste good. I need one." Dal smiled, taking one for himself and humming over it.

Oh, that would never do -- he wanted to feed Dal himself. Of course first, he wanted to lick the bit of sauce from the corner of Dal's lips. Leaning in, he let his tongue collect the drizzle, the mayonnaise and spice good on his tongue. Dal's lips themselves were a bigger temptation though and his tongue slid across them.

"Mmm. Am I on the menu?" Dal swayed a little on the chair, almost like the man was dancing.

"Indeed," he murmured, fingers sliding over the silk shirt again. "You're a lovely spice on any food."

He picked up one of the lamb sticks, rubbed it along Dal's lips. Dal snapped at the meat, teeth sinking in and making Dillon laugh. Smiling, he licked a sesame seed from Dal's lips and ate the second bite off the stick. Oh, this one was good. Humming, he picked a tiny hamburger up with his fingers and popped it into his mouth. He bit it in half before bringing their lips together, sharing the savory meat with Dal.

Dal ended up scooting over into his lap, both of them laughing and sharing the food, the wine, acting like they didn't have a care in the world between them. One course slid into another as they sampled from each other almost as much as from the plates. The flavors all melded one into the other, the taste of Dal twisting through them all, both salty and sweet. Delicious.

His hands kept straying, staining the pretty white silk shirt as he felt Dal up, fingertips searching out the edges of the cincher. Dal's skin was hot as fire, the leather squeezing it like an old lover, holding tight.

Dessert was finger foods like the appetizers had been: little cream puffs and mini-éclairs, the cream in them bursting out and painting Dal's lips for him again and again. By the time they'd eaten their fill he was hard and wanting, Dal's shirt unbuttoned so he could admire. Those tight little nipples were rouged, the bits of flesh hard for him.

"I do love the way you beg for it, baby." He plucked at the pretty nipples, utterly unable to resist.

"I didn't say a word, you know." Dal arched, teeth sinking into that full bottom lip.

"I know. And yet I heard you loud and clear and I *love* that." He did -- the way Dal's body begged for each and every touch made him so hard.

"Good." Dal had worked his jacket off courses ago, had unbuttoned his shirt. Now those clever fingers went for his pants, opening them up.

He groaned, hips bucking up. Dal made him so hard, made him forget all his careful plans. "We were supposed to dance after dinner," he noted, licking his lips as he waited for Dal's hands to wrap around his prick.

"Okay. I love dancing." Dal slid off his lap, kneeling before him and licking all the way up his prick.

"This isn't..." His words faded -- who was he to argue with Dal when his lover did that? They could dance later. He slid his hand through Dal's hair, moaning softly. Dal's tongue was hot, slick, making his skin tingle.

Those quick fingers were working his balls -- rolling and tugging, pulling just enough to make him rock and arch. Moaning, he slid his fingers over Dal's face, feeling where those warm lips met his skin. "Good. More." He couldn't seem to come up with more than single syllable words.

"Mmmhmm." Dal moved slow and easy, teasing him and drawing it out.

He bucked, trying to get Dal to take him in, moaning when he just got more of that hot tongue sliding on his skin. Dal's teasing was going to kill him. What a wonderful way to go.

The ridge of his cockhead was nibbled and licked, then the slit was explored, the tip of Dal's tongue just barely pressing inside. "Baby." The word was mostly whimper, his breath catching in his throat as his hips jerked. "Fuck."

Dal nodded, humming as those lips opened and took him right in. Fuck, yes. That's what he wanted, what he'd been waiting for. His hands wrapped around Dal's head, hips pushing his cock in again and again. Relaxed and easy, Dal just let him in and in and in, no drama, no hesitation. His hips moved faster and faster, fucking those lovely lips, Dal's hair like silk in his fingers.

He could feel his orgasm building, feel Dal's mouth demand it. Dal took him in all the way, lips tight around the base of his cock. He called out, cock pulsing, his come pushing down Dal's throat in sharp bursts. His hips kept moving, tiny jerks as the pleasure pushed through him.

Dal cleaned his cock, tongue sliding over his shaft. "Mmm. Good."

He hummed, fingers sliding over Dal's mouth, that tongue flicking out to lick his fingertips. "Do you need, Dal? Is your cock hard for me?"

"That's not new." Dal laughed, eyes just dancing.

"Neither is this," he murmured, pulling a black leather cock ring from his pocket. There were small studs on it, meant to go on the inside, designed to drive Dal wild. Dal's eyes went wide, lips forming a sweet, bruised "o". He patted his lap. "Come sit here again and I'll get you ready for our dance."

"You want me to dance with that on?"

"Mmm. I do. Leather wrapping your torso, leather wrapping your cock. Oh, yes. I do."

Dal groaned, sliding into his lap, cock a hard bulge in his slacks.

Moaning softly, Dillon slid his fingers over the silk-covered cock, feeling the heat of Dal through his trousers. "All for me." His fingers plucked open the first button, then the next and the third.

"Yeah. You. I mean, I." Dal blushed and shook his head, hips pushing up into his fingers.

Oh, so lovely. Bending, he brought their mouths together, lips sliding, nibbling, biting, as that heat slid along his palm. "Yes, Dal. You." He licked Dal's lower lip and wrapped the leather around the base of Dal's cock.

Dal leaned into the kiss, taking it deep and hard, that mouth still tasting like him. He squeezed Dal's cock, pressed a finger along the studded ring at the base. God, such a sensual, sexy man.

"Fuck me..." Dal growled, toes curling, pushing up toward his touch.

"Oh yes. Not right this minute, but it's coming. I promise." He gave Dal's cock one last sweet stroke, and then tucked it back into Dal's pants, barely able to do the buttons up around the hard flesh.

"Bastard." Oh, look at that fire.

"You don't want to dance with me, baby?" He pushed gently, helping Dal to stand. "There's music, low lighting..." He held his hand out, waiting for that lovely hand to slide into his.

Dal moaned and stepped right up into his arms, almost cuddling, warm and sensual. He hummed softly, giving them music to sway to, to slowly dance their way over to the stereo. He flipped it on and dimmed the lights, moving slow and easy with Dal.

It was easier than he'd thought it would be. More peaceful. Gentler. He could feel Dal's heat beneath the silk, could feel the motions of the sexy body beneath his fingers, and against his own body. It made him hard, made him need, and he hummed, fingers sliding to draw circles in the small of Dal's back, right beneath the edge of the cincher. Dal gasped, lips soft and hot on his throat.

"So sexy," he murmured, hands moving to push the silk shirt from Dal's shoulders. "Oh, yes, look at that."

"Hmm? Look at what, lover?" Dal lifted his face for a kiss.

Dillon chuckled, licking quickly across Dal's lips, and then stepping slightly back. "Look at you."

Reaching out, he slid his fingers along the top of the cincher, flicking them up as he passed the pretty rouged nipples, fingertips rubbing against Dal's nipples. White cincher, black pants with a prominent bulge, rouged nipples, kohled eyes -- Dal had put on his plumage tonight, and Dillon admired every bit of it.

"You're perverse, you do realize that?" Dal was trying his best not to buck, to gasp.

He let one of his eyebrows rise. "You're the one in all the leather," he pointed out, voice rather husky. His fingers repeated their journey along the edge of the cincher, this time stopping long enough to pinch the pretty nipples.

"Mmm. Harder." Dal groaned, arching against him.

He laughed, pinching one nipple, letting Dal feel his fingernails. "You're always so pushy, baby."

"I want to get them pierced. I never will, but I want to."

He groaned, pinching the other one, harder this time, his cock jerking in his pants. "You'd look stunning." He'd find clamps that looked like rings for Dal. And he'd have them made if he couldn't find them.

"You think so? I'd be crazy."

He tugged Dal closer and slid his hand down

the back of the silk pants, fingers sliding over Dal's crack, following it down to the little hidden rings. "Crazier than this?"

"I'm used to those." Dal leaned forward, lips brushing his ear. "I can forget them."

"Not when I do this you can't." He twisted and tugged one ring and then the other, working them with rough, jerky movements. "We could put a weight on them. Then you wouldn't forget."

"Not a chance." Oh, look at that pretty flush.

"Maybe not *this* time." God, he'd love to know Dal had a weight or two on during their next meeting. Something that was *his*.

He swallowed hard. "So, you still want a next time?"

He met Dal's lovely eyes. "Don't you?"

"Yes." The word was bald. Simple. Full of emotion.

He nodded, hand sliding to cup Dal's head. "Me, too, baby." He brought their mouths together, groaning into the kiss, the heat between them immediate, explosive.

Dal wrapped his arms around Dillon, hands squeezing hard enough to leave marks. Leg pushing between Dal's, giving that bound prick something to rub against, he fucked Dal's lips with his tongue, holding on just as tight. Every little rock and jerk made Dal whimper, made another low groan push into his lips. Those blue eyes watched him, just drinking him up. He loved how sexy Dal was, how *involved*. Dal never just let things happen to him, it was always them doing it together. He pushed his hand into

Dal's pants, fingers pushing at the ring, letting the studs do their thing on Dal's cock.

"More. Want to feel you tomorrow. The day after." Dal bit his bottom lip, making it sting.

He hissed, and nodded, tongue swiping across Dal's lips. "I'm gonna fuck you over the couch, and then I'm going to take you to bed and fuck you through the mattress. Gonna feel me for *days*." Dal wasn't going to forget him any time soon. After all, he'd had his hand inside that beautiful body.

"Good." The kiss took on an edge of desperation, Dal almost trying to climb into him.

"Yeah. Dancing's over, baby." He stepped back, hands taking Dal's, tugging his lover to the couch. He tugged the silk shirt off first and then leaned Dal over the back of the couch, hands sliding from shoulders on down, loving the feel of skin and leather and silk on against his palms. Dal's hips rocked, ass arching up and pushing toward his hands. Begging for it. For him.

Dal was beautiful, the white and black of the cincher and pants complementing the pale skin dotted with his marks, all of it laid out on the deep red leather of the couch. His cock throbbed, and he removed his jacket, hanging it over the couch next to Dal. "I'm going to take my time, baby. Make you wait for it. Make you crazy for it."

Dal's laugh had that raw-edged need in it, that sound he'd become used to, damn it.

Addicted to.

"I'm already crazy, lover."

"Crazy for me?" he asked, moving around the couch so Dal could watch him slowly undo his tie, remove it, before undoing his cuff-links.

Dal settled a little, hand disappearing behind the back of the couch. "Mmmhmm."

"Tsk, tsk. You aren't touching yourself, are you, baby?" He put the cufflinks on the coffee table and started undoing buttons. "Because your cock and ass are mine."

"Yeah? Prove it." Pushy man. Dillon fucking loved it.

Chuckling, he pulled his loose tie from around his neck and knelt on the couch in front of Dal. Grabbing Dal's hands, he looped his tie around them. "There. Now you can't touch while I'm busy, hmm?" He tugged Dal's head up and took a kiss, quick and hard, before backing up and shrugging out of his shirt.

"Bitch." Dal was grinning, excited, hips still moving like he was fucking the couch.

Dillon licked his lips, managed to hold back his low moan through sheer will power as his shirt floated down around his feet. "Anticipation heightens the palate, baby. Did no one ever teach you that?" He undid his belt, pulled it out so very slowly.

"Lover, my whole life is a study in anticipation."

"Then you should be used to this," he murmured, undoing the top button, then the zipper. His cock surged out, his own need more than apparent, and he slid his finger into his right pocket, grabbing a condom before letting the trousers slide right off his hips.

"Already up again for me? Impressive." Dal was cruising for a bruising, the grin on the man's face wicked as fuck.

"I've half a mind to plug you and leave you trussed and wanting half the night." And if it wasn't their last night, he just might have done so. But he wanted that ass, needed it like they hadn't just spent two weeks fucking like bunnies already.

"You and your plugs. You like that, don't you? Knowing I'm spread wide, aching?" No, no fair, fighting back.

"I like knowing you're ready for me -- that you can feel yourself spread and full and waiting for it to be me instead." He toed off his shoes and pulled off his socks, took his pants off, then leaned forward to whisper in Dal's ear. "Wanting it to be me instead. Needing it."

"So sure of yourself." Dal's shudder rocked against him, the heat between them strong and sure.

"No, baby. I'm sure of you." He licked Dal's neck and then backed off, moved slowly around until he was behind Dal, the black silk stretched tight across the lovely ass.

He slid his hand around, finding the front soaked, Dal's need dripping slowly from the tip of his bound cock. Dal bucked, hips pushing right into his touch. "Tease."

"No, baby. A tease makes you need and then leaves you. I'm gonna fuck you, then take you into the bedroom and fuck you again. And *then*

I'm going to let you come." He slid his fingers over the head of Dal's cock, the silk soft, but not nearly as soft as he knew the flesh beneath it was. "See? Not teasing."

Stretching it out, making sure Dal needed him so damned badly he'd never forget how much he begged for it, maybe, but not teasing.

"Jesus, Dillon. You make me ache." Dal stood, turning toward him, eyes blazing.

"I try, baby. I do try." He wrapped his hand around Dal's arms, tugged him in for a hard kiss.

God, that lithe body pressed up against him felt so good, made him want to throw all his careful plans out the window and just go at it. He wasn't going to; he needed to feel Dal lose it for him. Needed to make sure he was all Dal knew.

"Now." He turned Dal back around, bent him over the couch again, bound hands sitting on the cushions. "We do this like this." He undid the top button of Dal's trousers, and then the second one, making sure he slid his fingers over the head of Dal's cock, bumped it.

"Now. Now." Dal went up on his toes, hips jerking.

"So pushy, baby. So *impatient*." It wasn't easy, but Dillon took it slowly, undoing the last few buttons, and slowly tugging the silk down, knowing the soft, almost cool whisper of material against skin had to be driving Dal crazy.

"You've gotten to come since I did." Dal's skin was smooth, tanned. Fine-grained.

"Yes. And I'm going to come again and then again before you do. Gonna make you wait, baby. Make you wait until you just can't stand it for another second." Bending, he kissed the small of Dal's back, right below the cincher, the smell of leather and skin filling his nose, making him groan.

"Mmm. That's good, lover. Again?" Dal's thighs spread, just a little.

"Uh-huh." His tongue followed the flow of Dal's pants, sliding down along Dal's crack.

"Dillon." Dal leaned down, let him in. "You're going to make it hard to leave."

He hummed, the words making his prick jerk hard. He slid a hand to his own balls, tugging on them ruthlessly so he wouldn't come. His other hand slid around to jack Dal's hardness a few times. "It's already hard, baby."

"Uh-huh." Yeah, Dal was focused. On him.

He went back to his licking, finding that sweet little hole and pushing his tongue inside it. He pressed his fingertip against the slit in Dal's cock at the same time. Dal's knees buckled, the deep cry filling the air. That deep cry shaped like his name. His.

He slid a finger into Dal along with his tongue, his other hand still playing with the head of Dal's cock, teasing and pushing, fingertips scraping the sensitive skin. They found a rhythm, both of them rocking and groaning, Dal's cries getting steadily louder.

He finally couldn't stand it any longer and rose up, quickly covering his cock before pushing into Dal's tight hole. Dal rippled around him, almost standing straight up, muscles shaking. "God, you're tight. Hot. So fucking good." Humming, he started fucking Dal, his hand loose around the bound prick.

"I... More. More, lover. Fuck." Dal's bound hands fought with Dillon's, trying to get the ring off, get more sensation.

Growling a little he wrapped his hand in the tie, and tugged, pulling Dal's hands up to his chest and holding them there. "You. Don't. Get. To. Come. Yet. Gonna. Make. You. Wait." He punctuated each word with a thrust, his voice rough, colored with his own need.

"Dillon. Dillon, I... Oh. Oh, fuck. There. Please."

"Here?" He pushed in again, nodding as Dal's whole body jerked. "Oh, yeah. Right. Here."

Groaning, he leaned his forehead against Dal's back and wrapped both hands around the tightly drawn in waist. The leather was smooth as butter beneath his fingertips, but it had nothing on the silken muscles that gripped his cock, tried to keep him buried deep. "Feel so good, baby."

Dal rocked, rubbing the tip of his cock inside, driving them both crazy. He wasn't going to last as long as he wanted, but he'd be good for round two in the bedroom. He'd be able to last then, be able to make it real good until he let Dal come. His teeth sank into Dal's shoulder as his hips bucked, so close he wanted to scream.

Dal did scream, body bucking and begging, milking Dillon until he came so hard his teeth rattled.

Secrets, Skin and Leather

He half collapsed against Dal, gasping for breath, the skin beneath his cheek hot. "Oh, baby, I haven't enjoyed a dance this much in... ever."

"Uh. Uh-huh."

He almost grinned. His Dal. His needy lover. "You want more to eat?" He asked, circling his hips, pegging Dal's gland again. "We could have some dessert. You could eat it off my body -- or I could eat it off yours. Would you like that? I'll coat your prick with cream, lick it back off..."

"I'm going to hurt you."

"Oh, baby, you don't want to hurt me -- you just want to come."

He slid out of Dal's body with a groan, fingers sliding on the white cincher. "Bedroom it is. Though it would be a shame to miss out on the crème brulee just because you're impatient."

"Decadent bastard." Dal shuddered, stretching up and up.

"I try," he murmured, kissing the back of Dal's neck. God, Dal's skin was better than any dessert could ever hope to be. "You up for something sweet, baby?" Look at him, hoping Dal would say no.

"I want you, you beautiful, teasing son of a bitch." Fuck, that smile made him feel ten feet tall.

"I'm not very sweet." He winked, taking Dal's hand and leading him down the hall.

"No, but I want you." Dal leaned against him, squeezed his hand. "And if I don't get you soon I'll hurt you."

"What exactly do I have to do to avoid being hurt?" he asked, squeezing back.

"Make love to me."

"All night long." He pulled Dal into the bedroom and over to the bed, the sheets pulled down, ready for them.

Dal moved into his arms, face lifted for his kiss. "Please, love."

Groaning at the endearment, he brought their lips together, tongue plunging into Dal's mouth. Dal clung to him, the kiss going long, deep, Dal near stealing his breath. There was a desperation to the kiss, to their touches, the weight of their departure heavy on them both.

He tugged Dal down onto the bed, rolling on top of the lithe body. One leg wrapped around his hip, the other bent to nudge his balls. He slipped his fingers across the tip of Dal's prick, spreading the hot liquid dripping from it around.

"So good." Dal muttered into his lips, undulating into his touch. He nodded. It was. Dal was.

He wrapped his hand around the base of Dal's cock, pressing on the cock ring so the little studs pushed in. "Can you keep from coming if I take if off?"

"Yeah. For a bit. Yeah." That pretty cock was weeping for him, so hard, so wet.

He unsnapped the leather, letting it slide away as he rolled onto his back, bringing Dal with him. He bucked up, hands on Dal's ass, sliding their cocks together.

"Yeah." Dal ground down, teeth scraping his

Secrets, Skin and Leather

shoulder, the little gasp amazing.

"I want you to ride me, Dal. Want to see you stretched out over me."

"Want to feel you, deep inside." He got one kiss. Another. And another, Dal's tongue hot as fire.

"You're going to be feeling me for days, baby. Fucking days." He knew Dal would still be slick from earlier, so he reached for the condoms and slid one on.

"Good." There was a wealth of satisfaction in that word.

He rubbed his cock along Dal's crack. "Take what you need, baby."

"Need you. How the Hell you found a way in, I'll never fucking know." Dal almost sobbed as he leaned back, filling himself up.

"I'm Dillon." He pushed in deeper, hands sliding to wrap around Dal's waist.

"Yes." Dal nodded and Dillon thought he heard the man whisper, "Mine."

He licked his lips, watching the lithe body move on his cock, feeling the muscles inside Dal's ass squeeze him. His fingers slid up along the cincher, reached skin and kept going, intent on those reddened nipples. Those little bits of flesh tightened, calling for his touch, his fingers. He slid his fingers over them, then pinched, twisted, giving Dal more to remember him by. His thumb pressed into a mark he'd left near Dal's right nipple, tapping the bruise.

"Damn." Dal bit his bottom lip, hard enough to sting.

He jerked, prick shoving deeper.

"Oh." Dal stilled, shaking a little. "Right there, lover, but slow. Please."

"Want the ring back on?" he asked, hips slowing, just nudging Dal's gland this time.

"No. No, I want to come." Dal rippled, eyes rolling.

"Hold on as long as you can." He wanted this to last. Not that they wouldn't fuck again the morning, but it would be quick, fast and hurried. Tonight was theirs, though.

"I will. Go slow. It feels so fucking good."

They fit together like a lock and key, bodies moving slowly, coming together over and over again as he held Dal's bright blue eyes, staring into them. He'd never felt this. Never.

Dal's hands framed his face, fingers stroking his cheeks. Groaning, he turned his face, taking one of Dal's fingers into his mouth, sucking, tongue stroking across Dal's fingertip. A man could fall in love with that smile. The thought made him move a little faster, and he lost himself in the pleasure, in the feeling of his cock sliding in and out of Dal's body, the taste of the finger in his mouth.

"Close. Close, love. Please." Dal's eyes rolled, throat working as a dull flush painted his cheeks.

Moaning, Dal's ass working his cock hard, Dillon nodded. "Yeah, baby. Come for me."

Dal nodded, moving faster before stilling suddenly, heat splashing on his belly. The heat and tightness around him squeezed hard, but Dillon rode it out, waited until Dal's body

Secrets, Skin and Leather

loosened slightly around him and then continued moving. He bucked and pushed, moving hard and fast.

He tried to last, wanting Dal to feel it for days, to remember how good it was with him, but he could feel his orgasm building in his balls, the ache sweet. His hips jerked gracelessly as he came, a low groan torn from his throat.

"So fucking beautiful." The words were whispered against his lips.

He shivered, his own words given back to him. No one had ever... but then Dal wasn't anyone else, was he?

Arms wrapping around Dal, he held on tight, stayed buried deep inside the lovely body. He could feel Dal's heart beating against his own.

"Thank you."

"Any time, baby. Any time."

He squeezed Dal tight. Any time at all.

Chapter Seven

"Champagne is for pussies, Marco." Dal laughed, the lights spinning in his eyes. Thank God the holidays were ending. Business was slow; his personal life was...

Shit.

Non-existent.

He'd thought about going out with other men, but he wanted Dillon. He didn't want just some random guy to dance with at a bar.

Of course, what sort of a loser did that make him? To moon over someone who didn't even have his home phone number.

Still, he'd texted Dillon earlier, let the man know where he was going to be dancing.

Maybe, if Dillon was in town...

"So you want whiskey, man?"

"Yeah. A double. I'm going to need it tonight."

"Not celebra..." Marco's voice faded away, his eyes on the door. Lips pursing, Marco gave a low whistle. "Now there's a nice piece of work."

Turning, Dal's eyes lit on Dillon. Wearing black slacks and a black dress shirt with a button down collar, Dillon looked commanding. Edible. "Hands off, man. He's mine." He slammed back his whiskey and grinned, the copper and chrome walls of the club making the lights flash.

"Greedy bitch," accused Marco.

Dillon caught sight of him, a slow smile lighting the man's face. Sauntering over, Dillon leaned against the bar, not even seeing Marco. "Hey. Fancy meeting you here."

"Hey. I braved the crowds." *Just so I could see you, beautiful asshole.*

"Yeah, New Year's Eve always brings out all the crazies, doesn't it?" Dillon's eyes dragged over him. "Of course, that's not all it brings out."

He grinned and spun. He was wearing bright blue silk and the tightest pair of leather pants known to man. He looked *good*.

Dillon hummed, hand reaching out to wrap around his waist. "And what is this pretty plumage hiding from me tonight?"

He stepped right in, hands sliding up Dillon's stomach. "Just the same old, same old. Ink. Rings. Leather."

Dillon bent to nibble his earlobe. "Careful now -- you're going to make me too impatient to stay until midnight."

"What fun would that be?" *Oh, fuck. He'd missed that sensation.*

"Mmm. None at all, baby. None at all." Dillon stood back and grinned at the bartender. "A bottle of tequila, lime slices and salt, please."

"Yes, sir." Marco was almost drooling and Dal felt the urge to growl.

Dillon however, seemed oblivious to anyone but him. "Take your shirt off, baby. I'm in the mood for body shots."

"Pushy, pushy." *Fuck, that was hot.* "Where?"

"Well, seeing as we're in public... I guess I'll

have to make do with that dip in your collarbone, the sweet spot above your right nipple." Dillon's hand slid to his belly, found where his corset ended, fingers sliding over it through the silk before sliding back up to the top of the leather. "And right here. Now lose the shirt."

"Bossy asshole." He unbuttoned, laughing, nipples tight as stones.

Dillon laughed, the sound husky. "Yes, I am. Just the way you like me." Those blue eyes glittered at him, then moved over him. Dillon licked his lips, a low moan sounding. "And aren't you just the way I like you."

He spread his shirt open, knowing how Dillon loved to see him corsetted and held. Dillon's nostrils flared, one hand coming out to slide over his belly, stroking the leather.

"Here's your order, sir. You need a hand with that?" Oh, Marco was being a pushy little bastard.

Dillon growled. "No. He's all mine."

Oh.

Oh, Hell, yes.

"That's right." Dal smiled, heat flooding him. All Dillon's.

Marco held up his hands and backed off. "Hey, just trying to lend a hand, man."

Dillon just ignored the bartender, grabbed the bottle of tequila and the salt shaker. "Now remind me how this goes? I know it involves me sucking your skin... mmm. Does the rest of it really matter?"

"Salt. Tequila. Lime." He wet his collarbone

with the lime, salted it, then leaned back over the bar. The shot balanced on the hollow of his throat, the lime rested on his sternum.

"Baby..." The words was a low growl, Dillon's eyes going nearly black.

Leaning in, Dillon licked his collarbone in one long swoop, then he grabbed the shot glass with his mouth, head tilting up to drain it. Dillon tossed the glass away, the crash lost in the noise of the crowd. Licking from his throat on down, Dillon took the lime into his mouth, eyes meeting his as he sucked.

Jesus fuck. He couldn't be more in love with that son of a bitch if he tried.

"Another one, baby. I've got a powerful thirst." Dillon's fingers curled around his hip, tugged their lower bodies together. "Very powerful."

"Mmmhmm." He set another one up, stretching out, leaning back for Dillon.

"So fucking beautiful, baby." Dillon bent and nibbled the patch of skin between the top of his leather pants and the bottom of his corset, then nibbled all the way up along the corset. Lingering, Dillon licked along his collarbone, tongue sliding circles on the way to the shot glass. Dillon's lips wrapped around the glass, head going back in a quick jerk, the tequila sliding down his throat.

This time when Dillon grabbed the lime, he brought their lips together to share the tart juice. Dal pushed right into the kiss, tongue fucking Dillon's lips straight away. He could taste the lime and the salt, the tequila and Dillon himself, all wrapped together into an intoxicating mix. Dillon's hand rested on his belly, the other sliding to worry his nipples.

The kiss ended suddenly, Dillon gasping, eyes dark as they looked into his own. "Fuck, you make me forget anything else exists."

"That's probably a bad thing." He couldn't help his grin. Fuck, he felt good.

"Probably. Maybe that's why I don't want it to change." The hand at his belly drifted downward, Dillon's hand cupping him through the leathers. "I do love the way you look in leather, baby."

"Mmm. I wear it for you." Well, for them. For both of them.

Dillon kissed him again, then helped him sit back up properly, fingers lingering on his back, stroking, massaging.

Marco cleared his throat and Dillon's eyes flicked toward the bartender before returning back to his. "You want something else, man?" Marco asked.

Dillon shook his head. "No, I have everything I want right here."

"Yeah, me and a nearly full bottle of tequila." He stood, head rushing a little.

Dillon leaned in and blew into his ear before speaking. "The tequila's optional, baby."

Yeah. Yeah, it was. God, the man did it for him.

"Scott? Scott Daly? Is that you? It's me, Jack Hale." The voice wasn't immediately recognizable, but the name was.

Secrets, Skin and Leather

Jack Hale, playboy son of one of his biggest and most conservative clients, Patricia Hale. Jesus. It was a flood of icy water down his spine, and he tugged his shirt together, hoping to ignore the man, pretend that he didn't recognize the name.

Dillon straightened, keeping his back to the speaker, half hiding him from Jack's gaze. "You want to go dance?"

He nodded, cringing as the hand fell on his arm. "Scott! Man, you're a player? Mother would never have guessed. Christ. This is *hilarious*! Buttoned-up old Scott Daly the Money Guy, playing boy toy."

A camera flashed, then another. Oh, Jesus.

Dillon growled, grabbing the wrist attached to the hand on his arm. "Who said you could touch?" Quick as anything, Dillon had twisted Jack's arm up against his back. "And I'll take the camera phone."

"Fuck you, man." Jack's friends swarmed around, and Dal took the opportunity to back off, get his shirt buttoned and scramble for the back door.

Shit. Shit, what was he... Shit.

He could hear Dillon's voice as he fled, not the words, but he could clearly make out the anger in it.

Dal slipped outside into the alleyway. Okay. Okay. Taxi. Then home. Then out of town.

Christ.

What would everyone think?

Why didn't he care more?

The door to the alley slammed open, Dillon coming out, eyes searching until they landed on him. "Dal," growled Dillon.

"I have to go." He headed toward the street. God. His career. His lifestyle. What had he been thinking?

Dillon's hand landed on his arm and spun him around. "Who the Hell was that guy?"

"He's the son of a client. My biggest client. My very religious, very conservative client." He panted, in the midst of pure panic.

"Oh, fuck." Dillon sighed and ran a hand through his hair. "All right, baby. I'm parked in the garage a couple blocks over. Lets get the fuck out of here."

"Yeah? I mean. I shouldn't. I can't." He couldn't think. He couldn't deal with this.

Not now.

Not here.

Not in public.

Dillon snorted and grabbed his arm, started walking. "No? So you're just going to wander around the back alleys dressed like that and hope you don't get jumped or get pneumonia? I'll fucking drive you wherever, Dal. But I'm not leaving you here."

He blinked up, the snow falling on his cheeks. Oh. Right. Shit. "I'm sorry. You're right. I panicked."

Dillon nodded, moving them quickly through the people headed into this club or that, everyone trying to get somewhere before midnight. "I should have grabbed that bottle. You look like you could use a good hard shot."

"Yeah. Yeah. I could use a few." He shivered, arms wrapping around himself.

"We're almost there," growled Dillon, speeding the pace as they turned a corner. There was a sign a quarter of the way down the block, indicating the parking lot was full.

Dillon was right, it didn't take long at all before they were climbing into Dillon's Porsche. Everything was in kind of a blur of panic and cold and... "I. Shit." He settled in, hands scrubbing his face. "This wasn't how tonight's supposed to go."

"Tell me about." The engine purred to life, cool air blowing out of the vents and quickly warming.

"I'm sorry. I'll get out of town for a couple of months. No one will believe it." He could put his contacts in, hide out.

"You're right about no one believing it. I got his phone, made sure it was wiped." Dillon growled a little, eyes straight ahead. "I should have just texted you back to meet me at my penthouse."

"Yeah." He rubbed his forehead, head just swimming. He... He'd spent years hiding and then suddenly Dillon saw him and he wasn't invisible anymore.

He was taking too many fucking chances.

"So, come now. I've got good booze, a big bed, and you need to tell me exactly who this guy and his mother are, and what the ramifications are likely to be." Dillon's fingers curled on the wheel. "If I'm going to need to do spin control, I want to know before I need to do it."

God. He had fucked everything up.

Jesus Christ.

"Yeah. Yeah. I'll tell you what you need to know."

Dillon sighed, relaxing back into the driver's seat as they sped along the highway. "Won't be long, baby."

"I'm sorry." He reached out, one hand on Dillon's thigh.

"I know." Dillon's hand slid over his, squeezed. "I know."

That hand disappeared, Dillon turning off the highway, the Porsche just humming over the road, and slowing as they arrived at a high-rise with an underground parking garage. Dillon's home. How... apropos that he'd come to Dillon's home tonight.

They didn't live that far apart at all.

They pulled into a parking spot, and Dillon hustled him into the elevator, using a key to access the button for the penthouse. "Look at that, we'll be in just in time to ring in the new year." There was a little twist to the corner of Dillon's mouth.

"Yes. Lucky you, spending it at home."

"Yes. Lucky me." Dillon turned to him and pinned him to the spot with a hot look. "There's *nothing* we can do about what happened until tomorrow."

"Tomorrow's a holiday. There's nothing we

can do about it until the second." Except leave, and he wasn't doing that tonight.

"Well, there you go. Lucky me."

It wasn't until the elevator had dinged, though, and the doors slid open that Dillon gave any other outward sign that he meant those words. Once they were in the penthouse suite, though, he was tugged up against the solid body, Dillon's lips coming down on his in a hard, almost brutal kiss. Dal moaned and pushed up, hands framing Dillon's face, holding Dillon close.

The kiss went even deeper, Dillon's hands wrapping around his waist, holding him as Dillon's kiss bent him backwards. Yes. Hell, yes. He needed to know this. To feel this. Dillon backed him up against a wall, his back hitting it hard, one of Dillon's thighs pushing between his legs.

"You do anything special for me, baby? Cock ring? Plug?"

"No. I didn't know if you'd come. I didn't want to drive myself crazy." He didn't know if Dillon had other plans.

"That's okay, baby. I'll drive you crazy enough for the both of us." Dillon winked, thigh pushing and rubbing against his crotch.

"You drive me mad when you're not even with me." Dillon was under his skin.

The sound Dillon made was smug and self-satisfied and sexy as Hell.

Dillon took his hands, twined their fingers together and tugged Dal's arms up over his head.

"'Til I got that text, I thought you'd forgotten about me." The words were murmured against his lips, Dillon's eyes boring into his own.

"I can't. I want." More. He wanted more.

"Greedy man." Dillon nipped his bottom lip and pulled his hands up higher, stretching him tall.

Dal nodded. He wanted it all. Now. Forever. Goddamnit.

"I'll tell you what I'm going to do for you, baby. I'm gonna fuck you until you come for me and then I'm going to fill you up with a plug. Make you wear it and the corset and nothing else." Dillon moaned suddenly, body jerking against his. "I can't wait to see you like that in my home."

His cock jerked, aching. The niggling worry slipped out of his head, his focus on Dillon and that unending need. Dillon's fingers slid away from his, and both his wrists were held in one hand, Dillon keeping him stretched as the other hand dropped down and worked open the buttons of his shirt. He could smell the hint of lime on him, the faintest whiff of tequila from the body shots. He wiggled a little, pulling at Dillon's hands a bit.

Dillon laughed. "You're not going anywhere, baby. Except to my bed."

The hand around his wrists tightened to not quite painful, and one of his nipples was tweaked. Hard. Oh, fuck, yes. Please. He groaned, jerking away from the touch, leaning in to nip at Dillon's arm.

Dillon moaned. "Love that. How you're never passive." Grinding into him, Dillon more than proved just how much he loved it, hard cock rubbing against Dal's with too damned many layers between them.

Dal tilted his head, brought their lips together hard enough their teeth clacked together. Dillon's tongue fought his for dominance, fingers of Dillon's free hand playing across his chest. Pinching one nipple and then the other, rubbing him right where the corset ended, fingernails scraping over his skin.

He arched into the touch, going right up on tiptoe. Groans and moans filled his mouth, Dillon's hips pushing him into the wall over and over again, Dal's ass thumping out a nice little rhythm against the wall. He just let himself go, let himself move with it. Fuck, yes.

Dillon just kept pushing, kept humping and kissing and torturing his nipples, all of it sending him flying. It was like they hadn't touched in days, weeks, months. Which they hadn't. Every touch made the next one necessary, eager.

"Either take me to bed or fuck me here, love. Don't tease."

"Bed," growled Dillon. "That's where all the stuff is."

His hands were released, Dillon grabbing one again to drag him along. He got no more than a brief glance at Dillon's place: a sunken living room with huge floor to ceiling windows and loads of slick leather and black and silver furniture, a huge desk over in the corner, covered in files, a bar looking in on a kitchen on the opposite side. Then they were climbing stairs up to the loft, where a huge bed dominated the room.

"Like your house." He started stripping, toeing off his shoes straight away.

Dillon laughed, leaning against the railing and watching him, eyes like a fucking touch. "You can have the proper tour later. When your ass is well-fucked and plugged."

"You want me to stay that long?" He stripped his slacks off, the little satin pouch holding his cock and balls already stained with his pre-come.

Dillon made a noise, a groany, desperate little noise. "It's Tuesday morning before the business world wakes up." Dillon licked his lips, eyes caught on his crotch. "Undress me now, baby."

He reached down, hand slipping in to stroke his cock, the wiry curls tickling his wrist. "Why don't you undress for me?"

One of Dillon's eyebrows went up, then his face relaxed into a smug smile. "You'd like that, would you? Watching me get naked for you?" Dillon's fingers went to his shirt buttons, slowly undoing them one by one.

"I do. You're a beautiful fucking man." He leaned back, fingers just barely stroking, the sensations delicious. "I could eat you alive."

Dillon nodded, fingers sliding on his own skin as the last button was undone. "I think that's an excellent idea, baby. You can suck me off so I'll last longer in that tight little ass of yours." Dillon shrugged out of his shirt, nipples hard little points just begging for attention.

"I can do that. I'll suck your nipples, too, bruise them so you'll feel me later." So you won't forget me.

Dillon laughed again, the sound husky this time. "You're using my lines, baby." Dillon's fingers flirted with his belt, opening it up, but not pulling it off.

"They worked for you..." He couldn't help licking his lips.

"Oh, yeah. I seem to remember they worked really well." Dillon grinned and popped his button, slid down his zipper. "There something in here you want?"

"There something in there you need to give me?" Yeah. He wanted. Bad.

Dillon's hands moved away, the long, hard prick pushing out from the pants, red-tipped, wet. Oh, he could *smell* it. He stepped forward, without even thinking. Christ, his man was hot.

Dillon jacked himself a few times, pushing down his pants and stepping out of them. "All for you, baby. I want to see you on your knees in front of me."

There were times it was worth doing what your lover wanted. This was one of those times. He nodded and knelt, lips opened. Groaning, Dillon slid the tip of his cock along Dal's lips, circling them, wetting them. The smell was enough to make him crazy. Teasing with the tip of his tongue, Dal did his best to return the favor.

One hand slid into his hair, Dillon's breath catching. "Oh, baby. Fuck. Yeah."

He grinned, lapping and nibbling, just a little. "More?"

"Yes." Immediate and just a little needy.

The slit of Dillon's cock was wet and he pressed against it with his tongue, fucking it a little. A shudder moved through Dillon, the hand on his head tightening. "Don't tease, baby."

"Not teasing." He licked again, then started fucking Dillon's cock with his tongue.

"Fuck. Are." Dillon's hands dropped to his head.

He sucked hard, made Dillon jerk, then pulled back. "Not."

"If I say you are, will you do that again?" Dillon panted, eyes hot on his face.

"This?" He closed his eyes, sucking and pulling, demanding more.

Moaning, Dillon pushed deeper into his mouth. "Yeah, baby. That."

Dal sucked so hard his cheeks ached, hand still working his prick, jacking himself in time.

"So hot." Dillon held his head in place, cock moving in and out, sliding on his tongue.

When he looked up, Dillon's tongue was sliding along his lips, eyes glued to where his mouth was wrapped around the thick cock. Fuck, yes. He nodded, took Dillon in deep, lips wrapped tight around the base of Dillon's cock.

"Yes!" Dillon's hips jerked, moved hard and fast, fucking his face, giving it to him. Another shout filled the air, Dillon's cock throbbing, seed shooting down his throat.

He swallowed, groaning, cock hard as stone.

Dillon dropped down to his knees, bringing their mouths together. Yes. Yes, fuck. Please. Love. He grunted, hands gripping tight.

Dillon's hand wrapped around his cock, thumb sliding across the tip. "Want you."

"I'm yours. Please." Take me.

"Mine." The word went through him, growled by Dillon as Dal was manhandled onto the bed.

Dillon grabbed a tube out of the side-table, climbing up after Dal and spreading his legs open. He drew one leg up, begging for it. Needing it.

Now.

"Do love the way you beg, baby. Always have."

Dillon's mouth dropped down over his cock, two slick fingers pushing deep into him.

"Jesus!" He bucked, shot just like that, screaming his pleasure out as he came.

Dillon drank him right down, fingers moving inside him, twisting and stretching, curling and nailing his gland, making his cock throb and shoot a bit more. He melted, pleasure shooting through him in waves. Dillon kept him hard, sucking his prick and pegging his gland, refusing to let him go soft.

"Good." His eyes just sort of rolled. "So good."

Dillon finally came off him, making him whimper and try to follow that hot mouth.

The lube and a condom were place on his belly, Dillon kneeling between his legs, cock hard again. "Get me ready, baby. Want in you."

He nodded, fingers clumsy as he struggled with the condom, tried to get the package open.

Dillon wasn't helping, stroking himself, hand working that beautiful cock. "Use your mouth, baby."

"You're out of your mind. I can't even *think*."

"I meant to get the fucking condom open, baby. Tear the fucking package with your teeth." The grin he got was kind of wild. "Just hurry."

"Oh. Duh." He chuckled, tore the package open. "Right."

"You can put it on with your mouth next time." Dillon took his hand and guided it and the condom to that needy cock.

Fuck, Dillon felt good. Hard. Hot. Needy. And it was all for him. Dal got the condom on, almost cheering when he managed it.

Dillon didn't waste any time getting to it, hands pushing his legs up and back, cock sliding nice and deep in a single thrust. Oh. Yes. He reached up, hands wrapping around Dillon's shoulders.

Dillon smiled down at him. "So God damned sexy, baby." Each word was punctuated with a thrust.

"I try." He did. He wanted Dillon to need him, to notice.

Dillon's grin got wilder, the thrusts into him harder. "Works," muttered Dillon.

One hand planted on the bed next to him, the other grabbed his hip, rolling him up slightly. The change of angle sent Dillon's cock pushing past his gland.

His eyes flew open, entire body jerking and shuddering as he gasped. "There."

"Right here?" Dillon asked, pushing in again, hitting that same spot, only a little harder this time.

"Yes. God, yes. Right there." His muscles went tight as a board.

"Yeah." Dillon nodded and kept moving, taking him hard and fast. "Touch yourself. Pinch your nipples and feel up the leather holding you tight."

His fingers found his nipples, pinching and pulling, making them dark and hard. Dillon's eyes were fastened to them, lips open as Dal worked them.

"That's it, baby. Oh, fuck. Pretty. Sexy." Dillon's thrusts grew sharper. "More."

"I want rings in them. Want you to tug them." It was his new favorite fantasy.

A shudder moved through Dillon. "Yes," he hissed.

Reaching out, Dillon took one nipple between his fingers and twisted it hard. His cry was sharp, but needy and, God help him, he wanted Dillon to do it again. Dillon knew -- Dillon always seemed to know -- and those fingers twisted again, hard and right, making the sensation just shoot through him, straight to his balls. Then Dillon's fingers let go and moved to his other nipple, barely touching it, fingertip flicking back and forth across the tip over and over.

"Please. Please. Fuck. I need you." He sobbed as he said it, meaning so much more than right now.

Dillon's teasing turned to pinching and twisting, before sliding down over the corset, not nearly so hot through the leather. "Baby. Show me." Dillon's hand slid around his cock, tugging as Dillon went wild with the fucking, cock just plowing into him over and over.

There was no way he could hold back, so he didn't bother. He just humped up, eyes rolling as he shot.

"Fuck!" Dillon cried out, slammed into him a time or two more, and then froze, the cock inside him throbbing as Dillon's orgasm followed his own. "Baby. Oh." Panting, Dillon collapsed onto him, breath hot on his neck.

"Uh-huh. Good." Shh. No real life. Not yet.

They lay together like that for a while, and then Dillon slid out of him, disposed of the condom, and let his legs down. Dillon settled next to him, one hand searching through the drawer on the side-table. "We missed midnight."

"Mmm. Happy new year." He leaned, kissing Dillon's ribs.

Dillon chuckled, the sound fading softly. "Yeah. Yeah, everything considered, I think it just might be." Then a chain was dangled in front of his eyes, two little clamps on either end of the fine gold loops. "I know how to make it even better."

"You're an evil man." His nipples were already tight.

"And you love it," murmured Dillon, sliding the metal over his skin, letting one clamp slide against his right nipple. No. He loved Dillon, but he was fucking fond of the ache. His nipple throbbed, chest arching toward Dillon's touch.

Dillon leaned up over him and handed the clamps over. "I want to watch you put them on yourself."

"I could put them on you." He reached out, tweaked one nipple hard.

Dillon jerked, prick jumping, but he shook his head. "No, baby. You're the one they look awesome on."

"You sure?" He pinched one of his nipples, drawing it up tight.

"Oh, fuck, that's pretty." Dillon nodded, tongue sliding across his nipple and making it go even harder. "I'm sure. We're clamping these and plugging your ass, remember? I've got some champagne in the fridge. And I'll give you the tour -- watch you walking around with your ass full."

"You..." He pushed up into that mouth.

Dillon's laughter vibrated against his skin. "Me. You know what, baby? In the morning? I'm finding someone to come pierce these. Make you wear my rings."

"I can't." God, yes. Please. He wanted that, wanted to feel it.

"That's not what I want to hear." Dillon's hand covered his, bringing the clamp down to his nipple.

"I want to. I want it." He just couldn't.

"Good." Dillon's fingers guided his, closed the clamp over his nipple. Then helped him do the same for the other one. Soft and warm, Dillon's tongue slid around first one and then the other, the sensations warring with the harsh bite of the clamps.

"You're an evil man." Dal adored him.

"I try, baby." Dillon bit his bottom lip, turning it into a kiss and then backing off, tugging him up into a sitting position. Grinning at him, Dillon leaned under the bed and tugged out a plastic container, shook his head and pushed it back, pulling out another one in its stead. "Yeah, this is the one." Dillon put the container on the bed and lifted the lid, revealing what had to be a dozen plugs. "Pick one, baby."

"What all is under there, man?" And who all did Dillon use them with?

"Plugs, dildos, cock rings, clamps. A paddle or two. Corsets." Dillon paused, coloring just a touch. "I'm getting quite a collection. I want to see you in each and every one of them."

"I... A new collection?"

The corner of Dillon's mouth quirked. "I've been collecting for some time, actually, though I've added a few in the last few months."

Reaching under the bed, Dillon pulled out a larger box. When it opened, he could see dozens of cinchers and corsets in leather and lace, PVC and rubber, cloth and whalebone. They were packed with layers of silk between them.

"I've never shown anyone before, Dal." Dillon's eyes met his. "They're all the same size. Your size."

"Oh, fuck." He moaned, fingers sliding over

the fabric, over Dillon's hand and arm. "Love."
He did. He loved the man.

"Mmm... " Dillon's mouth met his, the kiss long and soft. "I knew you'd love them the moment I saw you in that club."

"I can't believe that you saw me. That you brought me to that... God, I want to go back there, love. You and me."

"Where, to the island? My beach house? You just pick the place, baby, and I'll take you there. But first you have to pick a plug." Dillon pushed the corset box aside and shook the smaller box, making the plugs shift and roll. One of them started vibrating.

"Oh, Christ." He reached out, finger trailing over the vinyl. It was good-sized and the vibrations would...

Damn.

Dillon's fingers slid over his. "Mmm... that one is wireless. I'd have the controller."

"You'd drive me out of my mind." If he was lucky.

God, that chuckle was sexy. "Oh, I'm going to do that no matter which one you pick, baby."

"There's make-me-horny and there's kill-me-with-need, Dillon." He stretched, wiggling his ass.

"So this one then?" Dillon asked, picking up the vibrating plug, hand wrapping around it like it was a cock.

"Yeah. Yeah." He rolled and pulled his knees up under him, ass in the air. He wanted it.

Dillon whimpered for him, hand sliding over

the globe of his ass. "Oh, Dal. Fuck. So Goddamned beautiful. Sexy."

Two fingers pushed into him, testing the stretch. He spread, balls swinging, hips tilting as he let Dillon in. Dillon's fingers scissored inside him, pushed deep, and finally disappeared. "You ready, baby? Ready to be filled until morning?" The head of the plug was placed at his entrance, cool and slick.

"That long?" Christ. That was insane. Luscious.

"I could make it longer." The tip of the plug pushed into him, then disappeared, then pushed in again.

"Oh..." He relaxed down on his folded hands, letting himself relax, focusing on his ass.

"Yeah, nice and easy, Dal. This'll feel so good, leave you stretched wide." Dillon's tongue slid from the base of his spine and down along his crack right to where he was stretched around the tip of the plug.

"Dillon..." He groaned, entire body shivering. Jesus. Jesus, that was hot.

Humming, Dillon traced all around the plug, and then took his rings in, tugging on them as the plug pushed further into him. It was like being in the ocean, the warm waves washing over him, feeling nothing but pleasure. In and out and in and out, Dillon slowly worked the plug into his ass, Dillon's mouth working a magic of its own all the while.

Oh, Christ. So good. So Goddamned good. He panted, rolled, acting just like a bitch in heat.

God, he couldn't think he needed so bad. Deeper and deeper, Dillon worked the plug into him. It wasn't enormous, but it wasn't small, and the stretch was delicious, slow and good. Then suddenly it was in, his hole closing over the base, his body so damned full.

"Gotta make sure this works," murmured Dillon, his only warning before the plug his body stretched around started vibrating.

"Oh!" He jerked, straightening his arms and coming up off the bed. "Damn. Damn. Dillon. Shit. I."

Oh, goodie. Incoherence.

The vibrations stopped, leaving him panting and wide-eyed, Dillon grinning up at him like the cat that got the canary. "Oh, I'd say it's working just right. Now all we need it a cock ring because I'd hate to have you come *again*. Your balls would ache." Dillon actually winked at him, and then reached over in the bedside table again, coming up with a figure eight piece of leather. "Holds your cock and your balls all nice and snuggly together."

"Mmm. It's beautiful." It was. It was stunning.

How was he going to walk away from this?

Dillon nodded, sliding the leather over his skin, tracing the edges of his corset with the ring. Even his clamped nipples got a touch before the leather was wrapped around his balls and then his cock. Dillon watched him closely as the ring was snapped closed.

"Mmm..." He arched, moaning low as pleasure flooded him. He loved the feeling of being held tight, of being caressed.

"Just look at you," murmured Dillon, eyes dragging over him, making him feel that look all over his skin.

Dal stretched, letting Dillon look his fill, letting Dillon admire.

"The whole works tonight. Stunning. Just..." Dillon groaned and leaned in to kiss him, mouth hard, tongue pushing past his lips.

His moaned "love" was lost between their lips, crushed in their kiss.

"You make me want again, make me need," murmured Dillon. He could tell, he could feel the heat and hardness of Dillon against his hip. Then Dillon moved again, pilled the pillows up and sat back against the headboard. "Dance for me, baby. Show me how sexy you can be."

"What?" He blinked over, just sort of staring. "Dance?"

Nodding, Dillon dropped a hand in his own lap, cupping and rolling his balls, fondling his prick. "You must feel every movement, every breath with all of yourself at the moment. So move for me, show me how the clamps and the corset and the plug and the cock ring make you feel." God, Dillon's voice was husky, his eyes dark and needy.

"There's no music..." He stood up, feeling vulnerable and open and exposed all at once.

Dillon chuckled, standing and moving over to a classy black dresser he hadn't even seen. There was a sound system there and Dillon turned it on, classical music pouring out of hidden speakers filling the room with the sound. Returning to the bed, Dillon settled again, licked his lips. "No more excuses, baby. Do it."

"Pushy." It was easier with other people, but not impossible. Dal closed his eyes, focusing on his body, the music, the heat inside him. He could feel the plug with every movement, the chains on the clamps swaying and making his nipples ache and ache.

"God, baby," Dillon's voice was like crushed glass. "Open your eyes and let me see *you*."

Moaning, he opened his eyes, staring right into Dillon, letting the man see everything. See how much he loved.

"Oh, fuck." Dillon's eyes shone at him, one hand sliding over Dillon's prick, working it with jerky strokes. "Absolutely stunning."

All of a sudden, the plug began to vibrate, shivering inside him. "Dillon." His hips jerked, hands wrapping around the bedposts for support.

Dillon moaned, the sound low and needy, coming in beneath the sensual sounds of the violins. "Don't stop, baby."

"No. No, I won't." He danced and shimmied, heart pounding. "I won't."

"So damned sexy. And all mine." The words were growled, possessive, Dillon's eyes roaming his body. The vibrations continued, starting inside him and going through his whole body.

"Yes." He stretched up, trying to take the vibrations in, trying to adjust.

Dillon nodded, hand slowly working the hard prick in his lap. "I could do this all night. Watch you move for me until the sun comes up and makes the sweat on your skin shine."

"I'll get tired." Sore. Clumsy. Sticky.

"You'd do it for me though, wouldn't you?" It wasn't really a question, they both knew it to be true. Dillon's grin was feral, his hand moving a little bit faster over that magnificent cock. "I won't make you do it *all* night, baby. But don't stop yet."

"No? You don't want my mouth?" His hips rolled, cock bobbing.

"I'm torn, Dal. I want to watch you *and* I want your mouth." Dillon's voice had taken on that husky, needy tone that made Dal's prick throb, ache. Groaning, Dillon grabbed his own balls and tugged on them. "Your mouth. I want your mouth."

He crawled up onto the mattress, hips still rocking, heart pounding. "Yes. Yes, love."

"Just look at you." Dillon moaned, tugged harder on his prick. "So sexy."

The chain hanging between his nipples got caught on one of Dillon's toes, tugging at the clamps that held him tight. "Oh. Bitch. Fuck." He shuddered, lips open.

"I'll kiss them better." The chain slid away from Dillon's foot, swinging gently.

Jesus Christ. No and yes. His eyes rolling, lips open, breath huffing from him. Dillon's fingers slid over his face, outlining his features. Between the swinging of the chain and the vibrations moving through him from the plug, the gentle touches to his face felt huge. His lower lip was tugged on, Dillon's thumb pushing between his teeth.

Dal almost sobbed, sucking and tugging, teeth scraping over that thumb, the salt of Dillon on his tongue. Dillon's hips jerked, his thumb pushing deep before backing up again and then setting up a sweet back and forth, fucking his mouth. "Damn, baby. How can I be this close again already? You make me crazy."

"You take a lot of Viagra?" He winked, both of them laughing, leaning together.

"Not Viagra -- Dal. No pill could come close to making me feel like this. No one else has ever made me need like you do, baby." Dillon wrapped a hand around that hot, hard prick and tilted it toward his mouth.

"Yeah." He leaned down, tongue sliding over the tip, just dragging.

Dillon's entire body bucked, the lean hips pushing Dillon's cock up into his lips. "Fuck. Yes." That's what he needed. He licked around the tip, head bobbing, lips dragging along Dillon's shaft.

"Your mouth..." Dillon groaned, hips continuing to make short, sharp thrusts, his lover obviously holding back, even as both of Dillon's hands cupped his cheeks and then slid back to grab at the hair on his head.

His mouth. Dillon's cock. Dillon's skin. His tongue. Whatever worked.

"Baby... oh." Dillon's hands tightened on his head, then let go. Then tightened again, holding him in place as Dillon's hips snapped up, pushing that fat cock into his mouth again and again.

He groaned, hummed, tried to give Dillon the best of him, all he was. All he had.

"Baby... Dal." Dillon moaned long and low, hips moving hard and fast. "Now. Fuck, now."

With a last jerk, Dillon's cock slid into his throat, throbbing and pulsing, shooting into him. Dal swallowed, taking Dillon in, holding on as long as he could. Dillon's hands slid away, his lover melting into the bed, panting a little.

"Come here," murmured Dillon. "Let me hold you."

It was the easiest thing in the world, to push into Dillon's arms, hide. The vibrations of the plug slowed, and then stopped, and Dillon eased the clamps off his nipples, leaving him simply filled, aching, held tight in leather and Dillon's arms.

Dal waited until Dillon's breath evened out, slowed into the heavy rhythm of sleep, then he kissed the strong jaw. "I love you."

He did.

Goddamn him.

Dal slid out from Dillon's arms, watching the man sleep. He'd hidden himself -- his true self -- away from everyone for his entire life and this man shows up and suddenly?

Bang.

Shit.

He had to go; he knew it. He needed to go and leave Dal behind before Scott Daly lost everything. He'd worked his way to the top by never taking chances. He couldn't afford to be stupid now -- not for himself and not for Dillon.

"I love you." He left himself say it one more time before going to clean up and slip out, taking only the pair of clamps with him and leaving a note that said, "No damage control needed. Be safe. Yours. D."

He'd be over the ocean before Dillon even woke up.

Chapter Eight

Dillon barked at his secretary and slammed down the phone. He resisted the urge to yank the thing out of the wall and toss it at the window across the room. He had more control than that.

Though a glance at the state of his apartment before the cleaning company had gone through it might suggest otherwise.

When he'd woken up with Dal gone, nothing but a Goddamned note telling to "be safe" on the pillow next to his, he'd been more than little pissed off. He was still more than a little pissed off. Two whole weeks and not a word from Dal, nor a sign of Scott Daly. The man's secretary was telling folks Scott was out of town, and she took messages. He had no idea if other people's calls were being returned -- his certainly weren't.

He'd even invented a work emergency, and still been ignored. He'd sicced his secretary on Scott Daly's, and he'd be damned if his pit bull hadn't come out of that with teeth marks and not a single shred of information. If it had been anyone else's secretary, he'd have poached her.

He'd been pissed off, sad, morose, worried, and was working his way back to hugely, enormously, gigantically pissed off. Who the Hell did Dal think he was, just leaving like that?

People did not leave Dillon Walsh.

Dillon Walsh did the leaving.

Not that anyone was supposed to be leaving, in this case. They were going to come out together and stop the rumor mongers in their tracks. But that took two. And he was sorely lacking a partner to come out with. Dal hadn't even given him a chance to put his plan forward, damn the man, hadn't heard him out. Stupid idiot.

Two weeks and Dillon had yet to examine too closely just why Dal's leaving pissed him off so badly. It wasn't like they'd spent a ton of time together -- a few days here, a couple weeks there, and a single night on New Year's Eve. He'd tossed lovers out of his bed in far less time, and with far less provocation than being outed.

Dal was under his skin, though, inside his veins, and he could feel the absence like there was a hole in him where Dal should have been.

The phone rang again and Dillon growled out a "what?"

"Mr. Gorset is here, sir. Your three o'clock?" Oh, butter wouldn't melt in Nancy's mouth, and Dillon made a note on his day planner to get the woman a bouquet. She likely deserved it.

Didn't mean he could help growling back at her. "I know who he is. Send him in."

Closing his eyes, taking a few deep breaths, Dillon stood and put on his jacket, did up the buttons. He met Gorset at the door, fake smile pulling up the corners of his lips as he shook the man's hand. "Bill. Nice to see you. Can I get you a drink?"

He went through the motions, working his

charm to get his company the best deal possible on this take-over. He'd been keeping his private life separate from his business life so long he could do it in his sleep, and before Gorset could gather a decent defense, Dillon'd secured an excellent deal. Of course, it helped that he had nothing to lose. To his company, this deal was just another deal, another feather in Dillon's very feathery cap. Gorset, on the other hand, needed the infusion of cash badly; it put him in a weak position to negotiate.

Coming out wasn't going to change that. He was in a position to call the shots. Sure, some folks were going to refuse to do business, but most were too smart to let a little something like who a man chose to sleep with get in the way of making money.

Damn Dal to Hell for not sticking around to hear that. For not caring enough to fight for them.

Well, he was going to find the man, fuck him into the mattress so Dal knew exactly what he was giving up, and then dump his ass. His breath got caught somehow, his chest squeezing tight.

"Walsh? I say, are you all right?" Gorset looked concerned.

Dillon nodded, forced himself to breathe, to ignore the ache in his chest. "Just a little heartburn. I should have stayed away from the sushi." He gave Gorset a wink and hurried through the rest of their meeting, assuring that Gorset signed the papers Nancy had prepared for them before seeing the man off.

Secrets, Skin and Leather

As soon as he was alone, he took off his jacket and loosened his tie, sitting back in his chair and closing his eyes a moment.

The phone shrilled and he yanked up the receiver. "I don't want to be disturbed, Nancy. Whoever it is, fob them off."

"It's Trent Reid from the Finders Agency, sir. He says he's got a report."

Dillon's muscles went tight. "Yeah, okay, Nancy, send him in."

He'd hired the man over a week ago to find Scott Daly. More than a full fucking week and every day the report had been the same. A brief phone call, and "I'm sorry, but there's nothing new to report."

"Trent." He only managed a tight smile this time, staying behind his desk and nodding to the chair in front of it. "You have some information for me?"

"Yes, sir. Mr. Daly is holed up in a very private resort near Greece. He appears to be on quite the bender, to be honest. Four days and they've delivered two meals and seven bottles of tequila." The man managed not to smile, but those dark eyes sparkled, the whites shockingly bright in the dark-skinned face.

Dillon kept his face impassive, his heart just racing. He had him. He knew where Dal was, and he was going to go there and fuck the man sober. And when Dal couldn't walk straight, then they were going to talk.

"Good work, Trent. Your firm has yet to let me down." He held his hand out for the report, glancing to make sure it had the directions he'd need to get to this resort of Dal's.

Nodding, he pulled out his private check book. "How much do I owe you?"

***

If he'd been growly before, two days without sleep and almost as long traveling had done nothing to improve Dillon's mood.

He waited impatiently for the boat to dock, the last hurdle he had to jump to get to Dal about to be cleared.

The first thing he'd done was book his flights to Europe, then he'd spent the few hours he had until the first flight dealing with business, clearing off his desk. There were still a bunch of open files, but he'd left them all in Nancy's capable hands. He had no clue how long he'd be gone, but knew she could keep things running for quite a while before anyone even realized he was missing.

He'd flown to London, and from London to Amsterdam, and from there to Athens. Not the most direct route, but it was what had been available, and that had to do. Then he'd driven to the coast and chartered this tub to get to the island -- the resort only sent boats for folks who'd booked villas and he sure as Hell hadn't booked anything. He'd be staying with Dal.

He jumped off as soon as they hit the dock and pressed a huge tip into the captain's hands.

Then he checked the directions his very

Secrets, Skin and Leather

thorough private detective had given him and headed along the path around the island, bypassing the main building where guests checked in. If he was quick, he could be around the corner before the guy barreling down a long set of stone stairs reached the dock -- the captain wouldn't give him up, not after that tip.

Fuck, the water was blue. And the island was green, with the whitest beaches he'd ever seen. He didn't see many buildings either, just the odd one, up more stairs, peeking out through grooves of olive trees.

Dal's private villa was halfway around the island, about as far away from everything as you could get, and looking out over the Mediterranean. And wouldn't you know it, it was also the highest point in the island and there were about a thousand stairs to climb. Maybe he should have tried the main house first -- he'd bet his Stairmaster they had roads up there and drove the guests to their villas.

Only, he wasn't sure just how fiercely management guarded their guests' privacy. Pretty damned fiercely was his guess, so there was nothing for it but to climb the damned stairs even if it took him the rest of the damned day.

The sun was setting as he reached the tiny cabin, just managing to hide in the brush as a couple of teenagers carried down a tub of detritus -- bottles mostly, muttering together about the strange man in the cabin if his Greek was up to par. Which it probably wasn't. He waited until they were out of sight, barely registering the amazing sunset over the water, or the way the fading rays shone off the white walls of Dal's little rented villa.

Once he was sure they were alone, he strode toward the door, still trying to decide whether to knock or just walk in. He ended up doing both, knocking sharply and then just turning the handle on the door and going in.

Jesus Christ.

Just the stench of booze was enough to knock him back on his heels. Then the sight of Dal, unshaven and passed out, bottle in one hand and papers in another, was just...

Wrong.

It was wrong.

That clenching thing happened in his chest again, his heart *hurting* from seeing Dal like that.

His Dal.

His.

His stunning, beautiful lover was nothing more than a pale, messed-up shadow of himself.

Growling, he kicked a bottle out of the way as he strode over to the couch Dal lay on. "Baby? Dal? Come on now. You've been hiding from me for long enough."

"Dillon." Dal frowned a little, eyes rolling behind those closed eyelids, one hand reaching for him. Jesus, the stench was... not pleasant.

Growling again, he hauled Dal up. "Where's the bathroom, baby?"

"Huh? I. Dillon? Love? Are you real or 'nother dream?"

"Oh, I'm real all right. You're going to find

out just how real in a moment." When he found the fucking bathroom and stood Dal under some cold water.

There was a small kitchenette off to the right of the main room and a corridor to the left. He headed down it, dragging Dal along. The first door he came across proved to be the room he was looking for, all white and blue tiles, bright and cheery.

Dal groaned, swaying, head in his hands. "Turn off the fucking lights."

"Get used to them," Dillon growled, twisting the tap to get the shower on. The fucking thing was the typical European model, just a shower head on a hose, nothing fixed to the wall. He dumped Dal into the tub, clothes and all, and sprayed him with the water.

Damn, that felt good, eased a little of his anger over Dal running away from him.

"Jesus! Jesus! Cold! Fuck!" Dal fumbled around, hands up, trying to get away from the spray.

Dillon was relentless, though, making sure Dal's head was completely soaked, and then Dal's body. He yanked open Dal's shirt one-handed, spraying the exposed skin as he tossed the sopping material into a corner of the bathroom. Dal could have hot water once he was with it enough to manage the soap.

He'd decided that he wanted Dal sober before they started fucking.

"I. I don't... Fuck." Dal stumbled out, careening across the floor to empty his stomach.

Dillon sighed, the anger suddenly draining from him just like that. Perhaps it hadn't been easy for Dal to leave. Maybe this drunken binge was Dal's version of throwing things and growling at his secretary.

Dillon added hot to the tap and left the showerhead running in the bottom of the tub before going over to push Dal's hair out of his face, to stroke a hand along the shivering, twitching back. "Okay, baby. It's all right."

"Love..." Dal flushed and dragged himself over to the sink, washing his mouth out and grabbing a toothbrush. "I... I... You..."

"Shut up, Dal. We'll talk later."

He worked Dal's pants off while the man brushed his teeth, the skin goose-pimpling as it was exposed. He tossed the pants in the corner of the room along with Dal's shirt and turned off the lights. "Come on now," he said softly. "Let's get you clean and warm."

Dal whimpered softly, nodding and reaching for him, soft incoherent words lost against his shoulder. He held on tight, ignoring the way Dal's wet skin was getting him damp. Dal was pliable in his arms now, stepping into the tub for him and sitting, the water gathering at the bottom warm now.

Dillon grabbed the soap and pressed it into Dal's hands. "Sorry, baby, but you stink." He gave Dal a wink, grabbing the showerhead and spraying the hot water over Dal's shoulders, wetting his head down again. Dal moaned, face lifted toward the water. There. That expression

Secrets, Skin and Leather

was more familiar, even if Dal needed a shave and some food and some Goddamned sleep.

And him.

Dal needed him.

He didn't even need to argue the point -- that much was clear by the state of the man.

He wrapped his free hand around Dal's, guiding the soap to Dal's chest and rubbing, getting Dal started. Together they got Dal shampooed and soaped, the hot water rinsing it all clean. Then they did it again, Dillon not sure how long it had been since Dal had washed.

When they were done, he tugged Dal out of the tub and wrapped one of the big white towels provided by the resort around Dal. Then he picked his lover up and headed further down the hall. "I assume the bedroom's this way, baby?"

Dal nodded, cheek brushing his chest. "I think so. I've been sleeping on the sofa."

He snorted, though his anger had faded, and there was no ire in the sound. "You mean you've been passing out on the sofa."

The bedroom proved to be neat and clean, an open window letting in a fresh breeze from the sea, along with soft moonlight, and he put Dal gently down onto the bed.

"Yeah." Dal frowned, shook his head a little and blinked over like he was trying to focus. "How did you find me?"

"It doesn't matter where you go, I'll always find you, baby." He stripped out of his own damp clothes and sat next to Dal on the bed. "You ran away."

"I knew there'd be blowback from everything. You knew it. I wanted to protect us."

"I was willing to face it with you, Dal." And it still hurt that Dal had run away instead of standing with him, without even hearing his ideas.

Dal snorted, rolled to one side and stretched. "But this way you didn't have to."

His hand reached out, fingers sliding over the pale skin. There wasn't a single mark there that was his, no corset holding the beautiful skin close. "Not having to is kind of hollow -- it means I've lost you."

"I..." Dal sighed and leaned, body reaching for his touch. "I don't want to be your sometimes fuckbuddy. I don't want to be always thinking about how many hours I have left to be..." Dal sighed again, curling into himself. "Damn it."

He lay down on the bed, touching, stroking. "Baby, I... I wouldn't come out for a sometimes fuckbuddy."

"And I. I didn't fucking intend to fall in love with you."

"You love me? You have a fine damned way of showing it -- disappearing, refusing to take my calls!" His arms wrapped around Dal, tugging the lean body close.

"Protecting you. Taking care of your reputation. Asshole." Dal turned, rumbling at him.

"I don't need your protection, Dal. I just need *you*." Protecting him. As if he needed anyone to protect him. It was kind of almost sweet.

"I." Those blood-shot blue eyes met his, staring for a long minute. "I'm fucking scared."

"What part scares you?" Because, frankly, his reaction to Dal's disappearance had terrified him. He didn't get emotionally involved, but there was no denying that Dal was not just a fuckbuddy. Hell, being willing to come out for the man should have proved it to himself. If he'd bothered to examine it.

"The most? That I can't do it. I can't keep being two people. I can't go back into the box. I've tried."

"So don't, baby." Here was the conversation he'd wanted to have New Year's Day. "Don't."

"But... But I have to. My clients." Right, so Scott Daly had the most conservative clients known to man. Maybe Mr. Daly needed to expand his bases.

"Your clients will have to decide what's more important: what you do on your own time, or making money. I'm not saying you won't lose any, but I'll bet your... my ass that most of them will stay."

"It can't be that simple." He almost laughed. Scott had been playing the fucking game so long that the man couldn't figure how to stop.

"Why not? Why the Hell not?"

"I." Dal looked at him, then shrugged. "I don't know."

"If you'd trusted me enough to have stayed New Year's Eve, we could have cleared this up already, we could have faced them all and made our stand and spent the last couple of weeks exploring every nook and cranny of each other's bodies." He leaned in and took Dal's mouth, showing his lover what he'd been missing.

Dal tasted sour, but under that was pure Dal, pure hunger. Love. Those fingers tangled in his hair, held him close. He rolled them, putting Dal beneath him, rubbing against the lithe body. There was no leather, no latex, no clamps or plugs or cock rings. Just the two of them and skin and need. Dal's need was just as sweet here, just as rich and it was all directed at him.

"Want you," he told Dal, nibbling at Dal's lips, fingers searching for one of those sensitive little nipples, touching it so gently before pinching hard.

"I'm yours. You have to know that." Dal looked so tired, so worn, but happy.

"I searched for you and found you and came for you so that *you* would know that." He slid his hand down, stroking Dal's prick along the way. It was that sweet little hole he was after, though, and his fingers found it, stopping long enough to heft and roll Dal's balls, to twist the little rings sunk into Dal's body.

That deep moan went a long way to satisfy something inside him, Dal eager for him, opening and wanting him. He didn't have anything to slick the way, but he pushed a finger in nonetheless, trusting Dal's need to keep the burn from being too much.

Dal groaned, mouth open, tongue sliding out to wet those parted lips. "Yours, huh?"

"Mine." He worked his finger in and out,

watching as it began to spark pleasure in Dal. Then he pressed in a second finger, stretching, twisting to find Dal's gland.

He rubbed his prick against Dal's hip, leaning down to whisper. "I want to have you without a glove, Dal."

"I never have before." Dal's lips were on his ear. "You?"

"No." His fingers stilled inside Dal, and he drew back, to look into the bright blue eyes. "I'm tested yearly. I'm clean. Answer carefully, Dal. I have condoms in my wallet -- I could go get one."

"You could. This. This means we're exclusive." Those pretty blue eyes stared into him, so sure. "I haven't been with anyone since our first time."

"I have. The week after our first time. Proving I didn't need *you*. I was wrong." He started moving his fingers again, eager now to be inside his Dal. "But I was safe and I haven't been with anyone else since because you and only you are *mine* and I don't want anyone else." It was a huge admission for him, a huge trust that he placed in Dal's hands.

"Yours." Dal nodded, hand cupping his face. "I want. I want to be yours."

He held Dal's eyes as he let his fingers slide away and spread the pre-come around the head of his cock. He lined right up, mouth opening on a groan at the feeling of that tight heat pressing against his flesh. "You are mine." He sank in as he said it, the sensation familiar, but brand new at the same time. Unbelievable.

Amazing.

"Yours." Those blue eyes went wide, Dal's lips parted. "Dillon."

He could feel Dal's body clinging to his cock, holding it tight and hot. He could feel it clutch his flesh as he pulled out until only the head of his cock was being squeezed, everything so much more intense. Then he pushed back in again, sinking deep and nudging across Dal's gland.

"Love!" Yes. Yes, love. Dal shuddered, bucked so that his cock rubbed the same place, again and again.

It have never felt anything but good with Dal, but like this. Oh, fuck, it was something else. Groaning, he let Dal set the pace, just moved with that sexy body, watching it writhe and ripple for him. It didn't take long -- it wouldn't, as tired as Dal was -- but as long as it lasted, it was fabulous.

He could feel Dal tightening around him, and he took Dal's cock in his hand, encouraging his lover's climax. "Let me feel you, baby. Show me you're mine." Dal nodded, hips bucking as spunk spread over his fingers. That tight little ass squeezed him like a fist, milking his cock.

Fuck, that was... Moaning, he jerked inside Dal and shot, filling Dal with his seed. Filling his lover with himself. Oh, that was... Whimpering, he collapsed onto Dal, nosing the warm throat.

"Love." Dal's hands were shaking, petting him, stroking his skin.

He kissed Dal softly and nodded. "Yeah, baby. That's what this is all about."

The rest was just so many fucking details, and as long as Dal didn't run away again, they could tackle them together.

Chapter Nine

Dal didn't know how long he slept, but he knew he was warm and safe, happy, held, and if it was a dream, he wasn't interested in waking up from it. Every so often hands would slide over his back, stroke him and massage him, ease him down toward sleep again. It was pure heaven.

At some point the hands were less soothing and more arousing, joined by warm lips nibbling at his shoulder, hot tongue lapping at his skin. If it was a dream, it was extremely vivid.

"Dillon. Love." He laughed, stretching out, feeling at home in his skin for the first time in days.

"Mmm." Dillon moaned around his skin, and then the lapping and licking turned into suction, Dillon pulling up the blood, leaving a mark.

His eyes popped open, the line between real and dream dissolving. Oh. Dillon. Marking him. Greece. Whoa. "Hey."

Dillon's teeth dug into his skin for just a flash of sharp before Dillon pulled back. "Hey, baby. Finally decided to join the land of the living, hmm?" Dillon tugged him back against the long body, fingers sliding over his belly.

"Uh-huh." Hell, he was even hungry, belly snapping and snarling against the touch. He'd run as far as he could and then buried himself in a bottle. In a few dozen bottles. It had all just been

Secrets, Skin and Leather

too much.

Dillon chuckled at the noises his stomach made. "There's food in the little kitchenette. You should have heard the shock in the girl's voice when I ordered it sent up."

"Yeah. I haven't been exploring the local cuisine much." He didn't know how much Dillon knew, but there was no way he was getting his ass into trouble.

"According to my sources, the only thing you've been exploring is the bottom of numerous bottles." Dillon gave his ass a smack and licked across the brand new mark on his shoulder. "You need food. And then I need to do something about beautiful, but sadly lacking in my marks skin. And this..." Dillon hummed, fingers sliding down to comb through his pubic hair. "You've still got secrets from me, baby."

"Do I?" Sources? Christ, how much had Dillon spent to find him? Just that thought made him ache a little, made him hot.

"You do. Someone shaved you once. Touched you here. Marked you here. I want to see it." There was a note in Dillon's voice, a growl that was possessive, not angry.

"I needed it. It was a dark time. I needed to feel like I wasn't just Scott Daly." He'd needed the burn and the excitement.

"You weren't. You aren't." Dillon's hand slid down to capture his balls, rolling them. "And now I need to see the mark." Another low chuckle from Dillon shivered along his spine. "Food first. I don't want you passing out on me."

Dillon's hand left his balls, the man's heat disappearing, and the bed dipped as Dillon stood, stretched, body long and lean, muscles flexing.

"Fuck, you're fine." He couldn't help admiring the way the Mediterranean sun made Dillon glow.

He got a grin, Dillon turning slowly for him, half-jokingly showing off for him now. "I've gotta look good if I'm going to be standing next to you."

"Flatterer." He crawled out of the bed, scratching his furry cheeks. "You like the unshaven look?" Christ, he was letting himself go.

"No." Dillon sounded pretty damned sure of that. "We'll get rid of it when I shave your pubes."

Dillon grabbed Dal's hand and led him out down the little hall and into the tiny kitchenette, bypassing any attempt at getting dressed altogether.

He laughed, the sound ringing out, seeming to join with the light. "What food did they bring?"

"Little bits and bites that can apparently be thrown into the oven to warm up." Dillon did exactly that, putting a tray of what looked like phyllo-dough wrapped bite sized treats into the oven. Then another tray was removed from the fridge, this one with little bowls on it, each containing something different. "Plus a bunch of cold appetizers so we can eat right away."

Dillon grabbed a big, black olive and pressed it to his lips. "Open up, baby."

Oh, Hell, yes. Cold and salty and rich and uhn. More. "Another one?"

"Yes." This time Dillon held the olive between his lips and bent forward to feed it to him.

He nibbled the end, then licked at Dillon's lips before stealing the rest of the olive. Dillon's laughter was soft and happy, the look in those eyes stunning.

"Octopus marinated in... well, something that includes olive oil." Dillon winked and popped a half-inch bite into his mouth.

"Mmm. Chewy." If it was longer, he could waggle it on the end of his tongue.

Dillon had a bite of one himself. "Oh, I like the spice. Subtle. Let's see what they did with the tzaziki." Ignoring the stack of pita bread, Dillon dipped his finger into the white spread and held it up to him.

"Mmm. Cucumber." He leaned over and licked the tzaziki off, humming low at the flavor.

"I was thinking more 'mmm, Dal,' myself." Dillon winked at him, and moved closer, reaching toward the tray, but holding his gaze.

This time it was a stuffed grape leaf that Dillon picked up, and once it was fed to him, Dillon's mouth closed on his, tongue sweeping in to steal a bit of the treat from him. They tried everything on the tray at least once, and then Dillon randomly fed him seconds and thirds, the tastes shared between them, each bite enhanced by the taste of Dillon himself.

The ding of the timer on the oven had them

both jumping, and Dillon laughed, rubbed against him. "Now for the hot stuff, baby."

"Mmm. Hot stuff." He waited until Dillon turned to stroke the fine ass. "How long are you staying, love?" How long could they hide here?

Dillon stopped, let him feel up the lovely skin for a moment before pulling the tray out of the oven, looking positively domestic with the oven mitts on. Well, as domestic as a naked stud could look.

"As long as it takes," was his answer.

"Oh." What was he supposed to say to that? He couldn't stop the smile that teased his lips.

Dillon saw it, grinned back, and then managed a sober look, shrugged with apparent casualness. "After all, who knows how long it'll take to talk you into coming home with me."

"Home? Home-home? Like, to your apartment?" Permanently? Honestly? Surely not. Dillon couldn't mean that.

"Didn't you like it?"

"Yes." He had. Well, he thought he had. His memory was a little foggy.

"Then, yes, home to my apartment." Dillon fixed him with a stare that looked right into him. "You're mine, where else would you go?"

"I don't know." He'd never thought about being someone's, about having a relationship.

Dillon nodded and Dal's hands were taken, the food forgotten as Dillon pulled him over to the couch and sat him down. "I have never asked anyone to live with me, Dal. I've never wanted anyone to before. People have always been...

disposable. I want you with me. Not just stolen moments here and there where we have to worry about who might see us. I want you by my side and if some uptight button downed assholes can't handle that they can take their business to the next guy. Who isn't nearly as good at his job as you and I are."

Dillon cleared his throat, a dark flush across his cheeks. "I'm not good at *asking*, Dal. But I'd like you to come with me. Please."

Oh, God.

Oh. Oh, he...

Jesus.

Dal searched Dillon's eyes, seeing nothing but truth there, but love and desire. "You're sure? I've never lived with anyone. I may be terrible at it."

"Baby, I wouldn't be here if I wasn't sure. I wouldn't have said anything if I wasn't sure. I don't say things I don't mean. And if you get on my nerves, I'll just gag you, plug you and tie you to my bed for a few hours." The last was said with a hint of a smile, but he could see how serious Dillon was, how the man was waiting for his answer.

"I love you." He hadn't said it sober, sure, knowing that Dillon would know he meant it.

Oh, just look at that smile, at the way Dillon's whole face just lit up with it, eyes shining. "Me, too, yeah?" Dillon poked him. "So say yes, already."

"Yes, already."

Dillon laughed, mouth meeting his, and the

sound pushed right into his lips, filling him. Oh, that was. Yes. Yes. He couldn't stop grinning, couldn't stop holding on. Dillon was still grinning as he backed away, that smile even bigger in Dillon's eyes.

"Bathroom, baby. We have some shaving to do. Face first, then this." Dillon's hands slid down his chest and tugged gently at the curls around his cock.

"What about your food?" He arched a little, easing the tug.

"Are you still hungry?" Dillon's hand moved to wrap around his prick, jacking him slowly. "Or were the cold appetizers enough to tide you over?"

"I..." His eyes rolled, that touch enough to heat him through. "I don't need any more food, love."

"Mmm... I can see what you need."

Dillon stood and tugged him up off the couch. Their bodies rubbed together, cocks rising to meet against their bellies. "Shaving first. You've kept that ink a secret for long enough."

"I had to keep you interested."

Dillon chuckled. "Oh, I think I was always interested in more than just the ink, baby. Way, way more than just that."

Dillon pulled him into the bathroom, the room so bright with the sun shining onto the white tile from the skylight. "This place needs a proper shower."

"It's something. I love the light here."

Oh, Dillon laughed at that. "You didn't like

Secrets, Skin and Leather

the light the night I found you here." He was given a wink and then Dillon bent over to put the plug in the tub, turn on the taps.

"I was a little tipsy." He had been drunk off his ass.

Dillon laughed all the harder at that. "Just a little."

There was a small box on the little counter, and Dillon went through it, pulling out shaving cream and a small package of disposable razors. "The staff here is really quite accommodating and even know a few words of English. Makes up for the lack of a proper shower."

"You realize those things will chafe, yes?" God, he loved that fascinated look in Dillon's eyes.

Dillon dug through the box and came up with an expensive brand of cream. "I'll make sure you don't chafe, baby. I'll take real good care of the area." Dillon licked his lips. "No more stalling. Sit on the can and I'll do your face first."

"No shit?" He grinned, sat, cock hard as a rock. "You know how to shave someone?"

"I do my face every morning, baby. How hard can it be to do yours?"

"If you cut my nose off, I'm going to hurt you."

"Then stop making me laugh," chuckled Dillon.

The shaving cream smelled good as Dillon sprayed it onto his fingers and then rubbed it over his face. This was no simple slapping on either, Dillon moved slowly, feeling up his face.

Dal hummed, lifted his face up, enjoying it.

Dillon's eyes met his. "Where are those stupid contacts, baby? I think we should throw them into the ocean." Dillon rinsed his hands and picked up one of the razors.

"In the top bureau drawer, along with my tighty whities." He hadn't worn them in days.

"I'm glad you brought them. We can dispose of them together. You'll never wear them again, baby. It's a sin to hide these beautiful eyes." Dillon tilted his head, drew the razor along his jaw.

He felt his cheeks heat at the compliment, loving that Dillon saw him, loving that Dillon liked what he saw.

One stroke followed another, Dillon slowly getting rid of his several days' growth beard. "Mmm... there's that sexy face."

"I want you." His cheeks were tingling, the skin awake and sensitive.

"Good. You're going to have to wait." Dillon grinned, looking down at his crotch. "Believe it or not at the moment I'm more interested in what's around that cock than the cock itself."

"You are so curious." He hid the skin with his hands. "Don't you want to keep the mystery?"

"No." Dillon shook his head, taking the time to wipe his face clean of any residue shaving cream, and gently massaging in some of the skin lotion. "Curiosity killed the cat, baby. You don't want me dead, do you?"

"No. No. We've just started, haven't we? We've just begun."

Secrets, Skin and Leather

"That's right. So lean back, baby, and I'll shave off these pretty little curls and see what you've kept hidden from me all this time." Dillon turned away long enough to turn the water in the tub off, and then came back, lathering more shaving cream between his fingers.

"You sure you want to do this here?" He spread and leaned, sucking in his belly.

"Are you kidding? No distractions, no phones, just us? I can't think of a better place to do this."

God, Dillon's hands were warm, rubbing the shaving cream into his pubes. He'd meant on the toilet, but as good as it felt, he didn't care. He hadn't seen the little chameleon in years, the thin tail just curling about the base of his cock and balls.

"Mmm... can't wait to see what's here, baby. Gonna see all of you. Every hidden bit."

Dillon's fingers strayed long enough to tug at his rings before his cock was pushed to the side, the razor at the ready. "You ready?"

"Mmmhmm." He spread wide, ready to let Dillon see all he had.

"Stunning, baby. Just..." Dillon licked his lips, eyes hot on him. He could see Dillon's cock jerk against his belly, the tip just leaking like crazy. "Okay. Here we go."

Dillon was gentle, careful, using a new razor every couple of strokes.

He watched for the first bit, then threw his head back and just felt. "Next time you do this, I want to be plugged. I want to be full and have you shave me."

The long stroke stopped a moment, Dillon groaning. "God, baby, you have the most perverted ideas. I love it." The strokes continued, Dillon nearly done now.

"The tail goes on my balls. I thought that was going to be the worst of it, but it just felt hot."

"It's you," murmured Dillon, fingers sliding over his skin, tracing the chameleon. "My chameleon. Fuck, I wish I was there when it was done, watching you take the needle on your balls, watching your eyes. Did you come?"

"No. I wanted to. I wanted to, but I didn't know the man, didn't want to embarrass him." He swallowed hard. "I came when they did my guiche, though."

Dillon groaned, mouth taking his suddenly, tongue pushing in as the long fingers stroked over his bared skin. "God, baby. Just. Fuck."

"Bed. Bed, Dillon." He shuddered, ass shifting on the toilet.

"Too far," groaned Dillon, mouth sliding down over his chest, making a bee-line for his fresh, pink skin.

"I want you to fuck me." He wanted that mouth on his cock. He wanted everything.

"I will. Through the fucking mattress. This first." Dillon's mouth bypassed his cock, going instead for his chameleon, tracing it, sucking on the skin where the ink was.

"Love." He groaned, hands reaching out to brace himself on Dillon's shoulders.

"Fucking gorgeous, baby." The tail was

followed, Dillon's mouth wrapping around his balls.

The pressure was almost an ache. Almost. "Don't stop." Dillon's answer was a hum, the vibrations going through his balls and up along his cock.

"Jesus. Dillon. Dillon, love. I..." Babbling. He was babbling. He started working his nipples, tugging and pinching, cock just fucking aching. That hum came again, Dillon's mouth just working his balls, fingers rubbing his skin, teasing his cock. He was going to blow, any second, hard enough to shoot the top of his head off. "Dillon. Please."

Dillon let his balls go, tongue snaking back over the tattoo before wrapping around the head of his prick and sucking, tugging, licking his slit.

"The things I'd let you do to me..." His head hit the wall, hips bucking up, fucking Dillon's lips.

Dillon let him, one hand sliding around his hips, encouraging the movements, the other pushed between his legs, Dillon's fingers finding his rings. It was all too much, the pleasure, the pressure, the need. He screamed as he shot, legs going tight. Dillon drank him down, mouth returning to suck and lick at his tattoo after.

"Sexy. Fuck. Dal."

"Love." He whimpered, skin so sensitive it ached.

Dillon looked up at him, eyes hot, burning. "God. Fuck. Want you. So fucking hard for you."

"Take me to bed." He leaned down, curling to

kiss Dillon's swollen lips. "Now."

"Oh, you get bossy when you're bare." Dillon's fingers stroked over his chameleon again before standing, grabbing his hands and tugging him along. Their laughter filled the cabin, Dal reaching out and pinching Dillon's ass.

As soon as they hit the bedroom, Dillon pushed him onto the bed, following him down and devouring his mouth, the kiss hard and eager, needy. He wrapped around Dillon, hips canting, going his best to get that cock where he needed it.

Dillon's prick bumped against his ass, slid up to glide over his newly naked skin. "Need lube, baby."

"I didn't come here for sex, Dillon. I came to drink myself into a coma." Besides, they'd done it last night without lube. Or a condom.

Dillon spat on his hand and used that to slick his prick up. "Need you." Dillon pushed against him, pushed into him, stretching him wide.

"Uh-huh. Yours." His head rolled on his shoulders, heart just pounding. "More."

"Yes. Mine. Mine. Mine." Dillon repeated the word with every thrust, eyes boring into him.

Dal let Dillon in and in and in, let Dillon take everything he had to give. They moved together, everything else fading away, not important. The only thing that counted was trying to crawl into each other's bodies. He cried out, over and over, loving the heat inside him, loving the way Dillon needed him.

Dillon's hand wrapped around his prick, each stroke sliding Dillon's knuckles over his sensitive, newly bared skin. "Now, baby. Together."

"Yes. Yes. Love." Together. His toes curled, hips rocking as he gave it up, poured himself out for his lover.

Dillon groaned and shook, filling him with heat as his body squeezed around that fine prick. Gasping, Dillon collapsed down onto him, moaning and nuzzling into his neck.

"Mmm. Hey." He wrapped his arms around Dillon, held on.

Dillon hummed, lips nipping his skin. "Now I know all of you, baby. Now that I see the mark you put on yourself, I want to mark you permanently, too."

"You want me to get another tattoo?"

"Maybe at some point, but that's not what I'm talking about. I want you to wear my rings."

"Your..." Oh. Oh, fuck. His fingers went up to his nipples. "You mean here?"

Dillon's fingers joined his, sliding and touching, pinching. "Yes. I mean here. One in each. I want to choose the rings. I want to be there when they go in, and it's my hand I want you to come into when they pierce your flesh."

His eyes rolled, lips parted as he gasped. "Please."

"Yes." Dillon's lips closed over his, the kiss heated, intense. "Mine."

"Yes." He squeezed Dillon tight, nodded. "And you're mine."

Dillon met his eyes, held his gaze for a long time before finally replying. "Yeah, baby. I am."

Dal smiled, nodded. "Then we'll manage."

Chapter Ten

It took him four days to find someone who'd come out to the island to do Dal's nipples. Well, it took three and a half days to make himself understood. It seemed that shaving cream and razors were more universally understood than "someone to put rings in my lover's nipples" was. Once the staff at the resort got it, they had the guy on his way in a flash.

In fact he'd seen the boat come in not five minutes ago.

Almost bouncing, he headed to the bedroom to wake Dal. God, he was nearly giddy. Good thing it was mutual.

Dal was sleeping hard, curled around a pillow, that sweet, well-fucked ass bare and right there. He wondered how long it would take for the piercer to get up here. Probably not long enough. He went over and stroked Dal's ass, fingers lingering, sliding along the warm crack, pushing against the sweet hole.

"Mmm... love." Dal rippled, ass pressing right back toward him.

Bending, he wrapped his lips right up around the skin just above Dal's right asscheek, sucking hard. He could smell the leather of Dal's corset. Not fancy, it nonetheless held Dal in tight. It had only taken him a little more than a day to get the staff to understand this one. He got a little squeak, Dal jerking away from his mouth, those beautiful eyes flying open.

He chuckled, licked the spot and then stretched out across from Dal. "A boat just arrived at the dock, baby."

"Yeah? A boat for us?" Dal's eyes were lit up, dancing.

"Uh-huh. A guy got off the boat. He's on his way here now." He slid his fingers over the corset, loving the way Dal's body heated the leather.

"It's going to drive me crazy; you won't be able to touch them for days."

He felt his lips pull into a pout. "Sure I will. "

"Nope. They'll be sore."

"I won't be able to resist, baby." He reached out, tweaking the nipples in question.

"You'll have to. No touching." Teasing bastard.

"I'll just have to cuff you to the bed, and then I can do whatever I want to you." He wondered how long it would take him to get the resort staff to understand that he needed rope.

He needed to learn Greek. Or take Dal somewhere he knew the language.

"There's no bedposts."

"Details, details. Damn, baby, anyone would think you don't want me playing with them." He pinched hard.

"I want. God, I want it. I've wanted it for so damn long." Look at his baby, that cock swollen and full and wet-tipped.

"Gonna get it, baby." He slid his hand along

Secrets, Skin and Leather

that hot, hard flesh.

"He knows you're gonna watch?"

"I haven't the foggiest. But I'm not going anywhere." He stroked Dal's cock again and thumb collecting the hot liquid dripping from the tip.

There was a knock on the front door and he grinned a little wildly. "Here we go, baby. Put on a pair of underwear if you want and come on out."

"I'm going to get dressed, love." Dal's voice followed him down the hall.

"Spoilsport," he called back.

He opened the door on a grey-haired... gentleman who had to be fifty.

Well, crap.

"You asked for a piercer, man?" The guy hefted a bag.

"You're American?" He wasn't sure which surprised him more, that this guy knew English or that the man was there to do the piercing after all.

"Ex-patriot, man. Am I coming in or not?"

"Yeah, yeah. Come on in." He stepped back watching the guy walk in. He almost had to remind himself to close his mouth.

Dal walked in, dressed in linen pants and an open shirt, looking beautiful. Happy. Excited. "Good morning."

"Morning. So who and what am I piercing, man?"

"Him," Dillon said, closing the door and moving to take Dal's hand. Just let this *grandfather* say anything.

"Oh, the pretty one." A grin appeared. "Cool."

Dal blushed, fingers squeezing his own. "Yeah? Dillon wants my nipples done."

"I asked for a variety of rings to choose from. I'm not sure it made it through the translation."

The guy laughed, still looking like a suburban neighbor in his beige slacks and white collared T-shirt. "It didn't. But I had a hunch. Brought something a little special."

Dillon shook his head. "I'm sorry. Are you *really* a piercer?"

"Don't judge a book by its cover, man. I know what I'm doing. I'll take real good care of your boy here. Make it good."

Dillon growled a little at the words, his arm going around Dal's shoulders.

"Lord, lord. Not like that." The man rolled his eyes and set his bag down on the coffee table.

Dal chuckled. "He's a little possessive. How bad does it hurt?"

"Can't say I blame him." Dal was given a wink. "It hurts like a son-of-a-bitch, but not for long. I'm Jacks."

"Hey, Jacks. I'm Scott Daly." Oh, look at that. Look at his Dal taking that first step. It made him fucking proud.

"And I'm Dillon Walsh."

"Well, all right, now that we all know each other, how about we get down to this. I need to get back before the sun goes down. You need to take off your shirt and I'm guessing you're going to watch."

"I am. I want to choose the rings first."

Jacks shook his head. "I only brought one pair."

"What?" Dammit, he was supposed to choose the rings. They were *his* rings for Dal.

"I told you I had a hunch. White and yellow gold, man." Jacks dug into his bag and pulled out a little bag with two rings in it. The two types of gold wound around each other, twisted together. They were stunning.

"Oh, look at those..." Dal reached out, stroked the rings in the bag.

"They are lovely." It was kind of hard to be ticked off that Jacks had picked them out when they were just about perfect.

"My lover designed them over the summer. Said I'd know when it was time to sell them." Jacks started pulling out his equipment, latex gloves, alcohol, a wicked looking needle. Dillon's own nipples tightened up in protest at the sight.

"Your lover makes jewelry?" Dal was watching with burning eyes.

"Yep. I won't pierce with anything else. Got a few nice chain pieces that might look nice between these." Jacks hefted the little bag with the rings. "If you sit on the couch, I can sit on the end of the table here, that'll be easiest."

"I want to touch him while you do it. Hold him." Dillon wasn't going to take no for an answer.

Jacks just grinned. "You do what you want, man. I just need Scott here to stay still while I'm piercing."

"He'll be still."

"I was still when my guiche was done. This should be easier." Dillon sat and Dal sat in the lee of his arms, leaning back against him.

"Oh, not a virgin. Good. I like it when you know what to expect. I guess I don't have to give you the spiel then." Jacks sat at the edge of the coffee table, knees between Dal's legs.

It made Dillon growl a little, how close Jacks got, knees nearly up in Dal's crotch.

The man was all business, though, snapping on the gloves and rubbing alcohol over the needle, the rings, setting one of the rings up on the end of the needle. "You about ready, Scott?"

It felt strange hearing Dal being called Scott while they were snugged together like this, Dal half-naked, about to get his nipples pierced.

"Yeah. Yeah. You've got 'em straight, right?" He could feel Dal's heart beating. Dillon let his hands slid over Dal's hips, fingertips reaching for the heat of Dal's prick, just not touching.

"I won't leave you lopsided." Jacks rubbed both Dal's nipples with an alcohol swab, making them begin to stand up, and then used a sharpie to mark them. "I need 'em nice and hard," Jacks told them, handing him an alcohol swab. "I'm guessing you want to take care of that yourself."

Grinning, Dillon nodded. Yeah, he did. He wiped his fingers down and took a breath, time suddenly seeming to slow. "My rings, baby," he murmured as he reached up to pinch both nipples

"Don't you make me come in front of a

perfect stranger, Dillon." The words were moaned against his jaw, Dal's head fallen back on his shoulder.

Jacks looked up at him and Dillon met the man's eyes. Jacks nodded. "I'll need to step into the bathroom and wash my hands soon as I'm done."

Dillon gave the man a smile and squeezed Dal's nipples again, making sure they were good and hard. "Do it, Jacks."

Dal moaned, tongue flicking out to stroke his skin. The moan when the needle went in made his cock throb. He watched, mesmerized by the way the needle pierced Dal's nipple, the ring threaded on the end just sliding right through. The needle detached, and Jack sprayed what Dillon assumed was more alcohol on the area before getting the second ring ready.

Groaning, Dillon just looked for a moment. His ring on Dal's nipple. *In* Dal's nipple. His.

Jacks cleared his throat and Dillon blinked, finger going to make the other nipple hard.

"Oh. Oh, fuck. Love. It burns..." Dal started to rock against him, ass working his cock.

He pressed his free hand against Dal's cock, pulling him in tight. "Sh, baby. Still now while he does the other and then you can move." Go wild in his arms.

Jacks chuckled, waiting on Dal to settle, needle and ring poised.

"Jesus. I shouldn't have agreed to two." Dal shivered and stilled, little ring throbbing in that freshly pierced skin.

"Can't have a chain with just one," Jacks said quietly, giving Dillon a wink before getting right to it.

Dillon felt Dal's body go tight against him, the cock beneath his hand throbbing, and then it was done, and two beautiful rings hung from Dal's nipples. Fuck, he wanted to play with them in the worst way.

Jacks sprayed the nipple and then got up, quickly and efficiently grabbing his gear and disappearing down the hall, giving them their privacy as promised.

"Love. Love, please." Dal pushed up toward his touch, cock throbbing. "Help me."

"I won't leave you needing, baby." He popped the top button of Dal's pants and slid his hand right inside. His own cock was hard and throbbing against Dal's ass, the sight of those rings, the scent of Dal's need, God, it was heady and arousing.

"More. More. Need." Dal was twisting, humping up.

He wrapped his hand around Dal's prick, jacking hard as he twisted Dal a bit more, pushing him over one arm so he could flick his tongue across the very tip of one newly-pierced nipple. Fuck. Fuck, that skin was burning hot, the blood throbbing in the little nub. He flicked again, lips closing over the skin. He ignored the taste of alcohol, concentrating on sending Dal to the moon as his hand worked Dal's needy prick.

Dal screamed, heat spreading over his hand, just throbbing in his fingers.

His own hips were working hard, rubbing his cock against Dal's ass, and the scent and sensation of his lover's come on his hand had him coming, too, mouth open wide over Dal's nipple as the pleasure shot through him.

Moaning, he brought their lips together. "You're wearing my rings, baby."

"Yours. Love. Love." Dal's head rolled on his neck, throat working. "Pay the man. Send him away. I need you."

Growling, he wrapped his mouth around Dal's Adam's apple, sucking hard for a moment before forcing himself to let go of Dal. His lover was right, get rid of the piercer so they could devour each other.

He looked around a little wildly as he got up, a throat clearing turning him toward the bathroom door where Jacks stood, looking down at his gear. Digging into his pocket, he pulled out his wallet and took out a bunch of American dollars. "I was told US funds would be accepted."

Jacks grinned and took the money he handed over. "This is a little more than the usual."

"Keep it. For making the house call."

Jacks saluted him, winked at Dal, and pocketed the cash, heading out the door just as easy as you please. "Left my card on the commode. You remember my name when you're looking for chains. There's some to match those rings."

"We'll have you send them." Dal's fingers traced the edges of his rings, moan filling the air.

"Goodbye." Dillon said the word firmly, trying not to be rude, but just wanting the guy gone. He closed the door as soon as Jacks cleared it, the man's chuckle fading away.

Turning, he just stared at his Dal. Cock still hard, hanging out over Dal's open pants, shirt open over the sweet chest, those little rings fucking stunning. It made him gasp, made him moan, his knees nearly giving out.

"Fuck me. Fuck me and then plug my ass and bind my cock." Dal reached down, started jacking off. "I need you so fucking bad."

He pushed Dal's hand out of the way with one hand, dropping his trousers with the other. "Mine. No touching."

Then they were kissing, mouths fused as he grabbed Dal's ass and pulled him in hard. Dal pushed him back and down, his back hitting the floor as Dal shifted, that tight ass taking his cock in deep.

"Fuck! Dal!" He fucking loved it when Dal got pushy – but wild like this, Dal was amazing. He reached up, unable to resist those pretty little rings. His fingers touched them, petting them.

"Yours. Yours. Love." Dal bucked, grinding down on him, the wet-tipped cock slapping his belly.

So fucking beautiful, Dal -- Scott Daly -- just shone for him, needed him. Made him need. He thrust up, meeting every downward drop and grind, the coupling wild and hot and so fucking good it made his balls ache.

"Mine, baby. Just... mine." He wrapped one

Secrets, Skin and Leather

hand around Dal's cock, that hot, silk heat pushing along his palm.

"Yeah. Just yours." Dal nodded, flushed and needy and perfect around him.

They moved together, bodies bucking and twisting, and he didn't want it to end, just wanted to stay here in this moment for fucking ever. It had to end, though, and Dal's body gripped him tight, squeezing his prick fiercely.

"Baby!" He cried out, hand working Dal's prick hard, his hips pushing up wildly as he came, pumping deep into Dal's body.

Dal nodded, coming for him, muscles taut and shuddering. He watched as the flush rushed up over Dal's skin, watched the lovely face in the throws of pleasure, and then he wrapped his arms around Dal's back and tugged him down, taking a long, deep kiss.

Love words brushed over his lips, pushed into his mouth. "Mmm... yeah, baby. You too. Love you, too." He'd never told anyone that before. Never said the words.

"I know." Dal smiled against his lips.

"Good."

And it was. It was very good.

Epilogue

The music throbbed through him and he started dancing, leather corset holding him tight, leather pants keeping him warmed up, loose. The little braided chain between his nipples caught the light, sparkled.

Rick and Adam -- the pretty set of twins that they'd met a few months ago on a cruise -- were on either side of him, Baxter looking on with an indulgent look on his face. Soft lips brushed his ear, Adam chuckling low. "You look happy."

Rick's long hair tickled his chest, lips meeting his shaved-head twin's. "He looks like he needs."

"Mmmhmm. Where's Dillon when you need him?"

"He'll be here." Dal leaned back into Adam's arms. "He wouldn't miss our date." Not for love or money.

Baxter grinned and ran a possessive hand along Rick's waist. "I wouldn't if it were me."

Dal laughed, patted Baxter's cheek. "No, you dear man. You wouldn't, but you have your hands full."

Baxter laughed, dark eyes happy as they took in the twins. "I do. I most certainly do."

Someone came in, drawing stares and Dal turned to look, and there Dillon was, all grace and elegance, walking like he owned the place. "Look at him."

Secrets, Skin and Leather

Rick laughed at him, kissed his cheek. "You love him."

"What's not to love?"

As soon as Dillon's eyes found him, his lover made a beeline toward him, face echoing his own happiness.

Adam waved, his deep voice ringing out. "We kept him warm and out of trouble, lovely!"

Dillon laughed softly. "Shouldn't that be he's kept you two out of trouble?" Dillon looked away from him long enough to give the twins a wink, and then his lover was right in front of him, eyes moving over him from head to toe and back up again. "Well, hey there, baby."

"Hey, love." He reached up, hands sliding around Dillon's shoulders. "The deal went well?"

Dillon's smile turned wolfish for a moment. "It did. I had them right where I wanted." Those big, firm hands slid along his corset, warm through the leather on his waist. "You are looking stunning today, baby."

"Thank you. I signed the Gregori brothers today." He'd lost almost all his clientele in the first rush of his new life, but in only a year, he'd found his feet again, found his niche.

Dillon had fared much better, but then the man always did have his fingers in so many pies, the big cheese and people couldn't afford to turn their back. "Oh, I had a hunch you'd be a good match with them." Dillon smiled, thumb sliding along his bottom lip.

"Mmmhmm. You and your hunches." He closed his eyes, head dipping to suck Dillon's thumb in.

Dillon groaned softly, the sound rumbling in Dillon's chest. "I was right about you." Dillon tugged a little on the chain between his nipples. "This is new."

"Mmmhmm." He went up on his toes, the tug luscious. Delicious. Perfect.

"Oh, yeah, baby. So sexy. And all mine." Dillon's lips suddenly crashed down on his. Dal cuddled close, the clapping and laughter of their friends like a wave around them.

Their lips parted slowly, Dillon rubbing their noses together. "You'd think they'd never seen two people kissing before."

"They just need more to do. Bax is having a big party for Valentine's Day. We're invited."

Dillon moved to stand behind him, tugging him in to rest against the long body. "Is there a theme? I mean besides the obvious hearts and candies?"

"Angels and devils. I was thinking I could be the devil incarnate."

Dillon's eyes suddenly went dark. "Oh, baby... little horns... a plug with a tail attached."

His laugh rang out, Dillon spinning him around under the lights. "You find it, I'll wear it." Baxter's parties were incredibly exclusive, even for them.

"I'll find it, baby," Dillon whispered into his ear. "Even if I have to make it myself."

They spun onto the dance floor, Dillon slowly working them across it toward the bar. "What are you drinking tonight, baby?"

"Mmm. Rick bought me a vodka and tonic. Lots of lime."

"He trying to get you drunk?" Dillon asked, growling a little, glaring in the general direction of Baxter and the twins. Possessive asshole. His possessive asshole.

"Maybe. It didn't work." He knew where he belonged. Who he wanted.

"No, I don't expect it would. Can't say I blame him." Dillon slid onto a stool at the bar, tugging him to rest between the spread legs. "Every man in here wants you. Too bad for them."

"Mmmhmm." He leaned against Dillon, letting his lover hold his weight. "The only question is, do you want me?"

"Baby, that's not a question. That's never a question." Dillon tugged him in closer, letting him feel the hard bulge beneath Dillon's pants.

"Well, then. We're golden." His fingers slid around to the small of Dillon's back, tracing the ink there by memory. Two stylized, joined D's.

Dillon's eyes went to half mast, back pushing into his hand. "Why aren't we at home where I can fuck you through the floor?"

"Because you wanted to dance. Because you like knowing I'm here and available." Dal grinned, stole another kiss. "Because Baxter asked you and you're his friend."

"All true." Dillon pouted. "I still want to fuck you through the floor." Over a year of openly being together and Dillon still wanted him, needed him like they still only had stolen moments here and there.

He let his tongue drag along Dillon's bottom lip. "Good. After dinner, you can fuck me in the car on the way to the beach house." He'd planned a long weekend for them.

A shudder moved through Dillon's body. "Okay." Dillon's mouth captured his tongue, sucking it in. Heat flooded him in a rush, lights sparking behind his eyes. Still so good. So right.

Dal laughed as he stepped back, one hand held out. "One dance and then we'll go eat." Dillon nodded, eyes on him, hand slipping slowly into his.

When they were on the dance floor, Dillon's arms wrapped around him, the two of them moving to the music, Dillon murmured. "I found a new wand, baby. This one gives little electrical shocks. Nothing too painful, just kind of... jolting."

"Yeah?" Fuck, he loved playing with this man. "Do you have it to bring to the beach house? We've got four days..." Four days, two willing men, and one winter storm promising snow.

The math was perfect.

"Oh, so that's what you've been up to..." Dillon's eyes were hot, smiling down at him. "It's still in the package it came in at my office. Nancy can re-address it up and express it there tomorrow. Don't worry, baby. She won't have a clue what's in the box. The company I got it from is very discreet."

"Perfect." He pushed further into Dillon's arms, the music going slow and sultry. "The twins want Italian. We've got a table at Vincenzo's."

Dillon moved with him, the hard cock beneath Dillon's slacks pushing at his hip. "They're more spoiled than you are." Dillon laughed softly, hand sliding on his ass. "They're more trouble, too." He could tell though, by the way Dillon's hands moved on him that his lover wasn't really thinking about the twins. Or dinner.

"I am no trouble at all." He was more... a challenge. Yeah, he liked that. When Dillon stopped laughing, he leaned close, lips on Dillon's jaw. "Of course, you haven't kidnapped me in far too long, lover. I would hate for you to lose your touch."

Dillon groaned, body jerking against his. "Something tells me you might be waylaid on your way to Vincenzo's, baby."

"Promise?" The look and kiss he received did more than that, Dillon stealing his breath, his good sense. His heart.

"Well, well, are you two selling tickets or is this a free show? Should I bring my mother?" The voice was snide, and he knew he'd heard it before, in fact unless he was mistaken it belonged to Jack Hale, the son of a bitch who'd stumbled across them on New Year's Eve over a year ago.

Dal looked over and rolled his eyes, then he laughed, Dillon's arms strong around him. "Bring who you'd like, honey. I'm busy. Shoo."

Over a year ago this man had sent him running in fear, worried his careful life was going to blow up in his face. Well, it had, but in the end, that had given him everything he wanted. And this time, Jack Hale was barely a blip on his radar. Dillon's arm guided him, his lover leading him from the dance floor toward Baxter, no doubt to warn their friend he might be a guest or two short for his dinner reservations.

"Hey! She thinks you're a sick perv, you know!"

"Which makes her think he's what, exactly?" Dillon murmured into his ear, otherwise completely ignoring the man. "He can't hurt us, baby."

Dal met his lover's eyes, seeing his own blue eyes just shining in them. "I know."

End

Secrets, Skin and Leather

Printed in the United States
84439LV00001B/36/A